AF444528

THE RISE OF A DOPE BOY CHICK

SHONTAIYE MOORE

The Rise Of A Dope Boy Chick

Copyright © 2020 by Shontaiye Moore

All rights reserved.

Published in the United States of America.

All rights reserved. No part of this publication may be reproduced, distributed, or transmitted in any form or by any means, including photocopying, recording, or other electronic or mechanical methods, without the prior written permission of the publisher, except in the case of brief quotations embodied in critical reviews and certain other noncommercial uses permitted by copyright law. For permission requests, please contact: www.colehartsignature.com

This is a work of fiction. Names, characters, places, and incidents either are the products of the author's imagination or are used fictitiously. Any resemblance of actual persons, living or dead, businesses, companies, events, or locales is entirely coincidental. The publisher does not have any control and does not assume any responsibility for author or third-party websites or their content.

The unauthorized reproduction or distribution of this copyrighted work is a crime punishable by law. No part of the book may be scanned, uploaded to or downloaded from file sharing sites, or distributed in any other way via the Internet or any other means, electronic, or print, without the publisher's permission. Criminal copyright infringement, including infringement without monetary gain, is investigated by the FBI and is punishable by up to five years in federal prison and a fine of $250,000 (www.fbi.gov/ipr/).

This book is licensed for your personal enjoyment only. Thank you for respecting the author's work.

Published by Cole Hart Signature, LLC.

Mailing List

To stay up to date on new releases, plus get information on contests, sneak peeks, and more,

Go To The Website Below...

www.colehartsignature.com

TEXTING LIST

To stay up to date on new releases, plus get exclusive information on contests, sneak peeks, and more...

Text ColeHartSig to (855)231-5230

1

Asia dug both her hands to the very bottom of her bag; ran them along the sides, and for the second and final time, proceeded to dig feverishly through the folds of her leather wallet. Still the same results. *Nothing.* Not one single fucking dime in place where she had left it.

"Who the fuck been in my purse!" she screamed out, startling, and inadvertently waking her one-year-old son, Hasan. The look on his usually round, handsome face was now one of shock, mixed with a twinge of fear. He immediately began to cry.

Damn, she thought to herself. She couldn't even go ape shit like she really wanted to. Had it been two years back, before her son was born … Let's just say, *it wouldn't be pretty.* She would have turned the whole house upside down to search for her shit. These days, she was no longer able to do that since she had nowhere else to go if her mother put her out. Unfortunately, her mother was notorious for that; and with a small child, Asia couldn't risk it. She inhaled a deep breath and exhaled it sharply.

"I'm sorry baby. Mommy didn't mean to scare you," she said

softly, before tossing her useless purse back down on the chipped-up, brown wooden chest that sat in the corner of her dark, tiny room.

Her lip quivering and her eyes brimmed with tears, she walked over and plopped down on the edge of her twin-size bed in frustration. The weight of her 180-pound body on the flimsy, pawn-shop mattress, caused it to sink downward, while the outline of several metal springs pushed against the material in an effort to force their way through. The bed groaned loudly as she leaned over and scooped her son into her arms, to calm and console him the best she could, considering the circumstances. She grabbed the blanket he had been laying on and covered him up with it; pulling it to his neck to ensure he was warm.

As she tenderly rocked her son back and forth in her arms, she leaned down and planted a few kisses on his chubby face for added comfort. It didn't take more than a minute to pass before the thick lashes on his eyes began to flutter and eventually close. Hearing his heavy breath fill the silent room, she looked back down and admired her boy. He was nothing short of perfection; hands down, one of her greatest achievements. However, at only the tender age of twenty-one, she still couldn't help but feel like a failure. How could she call herself a mother when she couldn't even provide her little guy with the necessities? Like a *real* mother should. She felt like she was doing the best she could; however lately, nothing seemed to be working out for her.

After searching for a job for nearly two weeks, she'd finally landed an interview at the Shoprite around the corner. It only paid minimum wage, but it was better than nothing. As broke as she was, she damn sure wasn't going to complain. Her interview was in one hour and she wasn't sure if she was going to make it. Although the market was within walking distance, she had to drag her son way over to the other side of town, since her mother had already said she wasn't watching any babies. It wasn't like she would have been her first pick anyway, and Asia didn't feel comfortable leaving her son with anyone who didn't really want to watch him. Besides, she hadn't even been a good mother to her. For that reason, she wasn't particularly confident in her grandparenting abilities. Nevertheless, she needed the help. She needed someone to look after him so she could secure a job and make some money.

Thoughts about her misfortunes caused the overwhelming sensation of despair to immediately hit Asia like an uppercut to the midsection. She looked around at her drab and outdated surroundings. The walls were dingy; covered by a lead-based paint. The once tan carpet was now visibly stained, caked with layers of dirt, causing it to appear darker brown in color. There was no way this was God's divine plan for her. If it was, he needed to go back into his study room and rethink that shit. She couldn't live like this. She was fed up, tired, and just plain disgusted by her life and current living situation. Asia peered out the folds of the dirty white, vinyl mini blinds hanging on her window. Although sunlight spilled through, to Asia, it might as well have been darkness, since there was nothing bright about what she saw. Trash, beat-up automobiles, and poverty-stricken individuals were the only images her eyes registered.

Asia loathed living with her mother. Loathed was more of an understatement. Although her mother had a three bedroom, it was smack dab in the hood; nestled down the street from a drug and crime infested apartment complex. Asia did her best not to go out much; choosing to stay cooped up in her room with her son. Her room was the smallest in the house, with barely enough space for a small bed and dresser. Despite all those things, she was thankful she had a place to stay. However, her biggest gripe was that she was sick and tired of mother-fuckers stealing from her. The hardest part was being forced to turn the other cheek in order to keep a roof over her and her son's head.

Her mother would always say, "You can't prove who took it. Stop leaving ya stuff around," but Asia didn't understand how money stuffed in *her* purse, that was way inside *her* room, could be considered left around. They all knew who the culprit was; her mother had raised him. Despite the facts, Asia said nothing to stay on her mother's good side.

The couple hundred dollars in her purse, had been her last. She had no idea what she was going to do now. She stared up at the faded, yellow ceiling, with its popcorn-cluster texture and thought to herself, *this would never be happening if my baby's father, Mitch, was still home.* Asia quickly stopped herself. Mitch wasn't home, and he wasn't going to be anytime soon. So, there was no need to keep sitting around wishing things were how they weren't.

Mitch was locked away in a state prison, hours away in racist-ass Coal Township, Pennsylvania, doing a twenty-to-thirty-year sentence for aggravated assault. He'd only been gone ten months, but to Asia, it felt like an eternity. Mitch was a money-maker when he was home; doing his thing down in Southwest Philly. Unfortunately for him, everyone from those parts knew it as well. Although family-oriented, he was flashy and had a reputation of being boastful. Under the watchful eyes of haters disguised as friends, he eventually became the victim of a robbery attempt in his own neighborhood. In defense, he drew his gun and let that bitch rip, injuring quite a few people in the process. Even some innocent bystanders. Although his absence was devastating and had Asia sick, she couldn't blame his actions. In the streets, the wins eventually came with losses. Real bitches understood the concept. So, here she was, back on the same shitty ass block in Germantown that she grew up on. The one she'd sworn she'd never return to. Living with her mother, and her thieving ass younger brother.

Asia looked back down in her lap. Feeling her son squirm gently brought her out of her thoughts. Looking at his little baby eyes flutter, and his precious face scrunch up, reminded her that she had to get up off her ass. She was now flat broke, and the soggy, swollen diaper he had on, was one of the last ones he had. She didn't have time to sit around and cry. There were moves to be made.

Laying her baby back down on the bed, Asia hopped up and snatched her North Face jacket down from the metal garment rack where she kept her small selection of clothes. She also grabbed her now empty purse and threw it over her shoulder. She had to find a way to drop Hasan off to his other grandmother and get to her interview. With a son to support, there was no way she could stay broke.

"Excuse me," Asia mumbled as she pushed past and strategically stepped around the morning herd of drug dealers and alcoholics sitting on the steps at her feet.

Like the loose pieces of debris and trash scattered about, they too littered the perimeter of the three-story apartment building she resided in with the rest of her family. Day or night, she couldn't walk outside without seeing one of their scruffy, or toothless, ass faces. Even if it was just running trash to the dumpsters in the back. It wasn't uncommon to see someone back there, ass hanging out, crouched down low in a squat taking a piss. *Or* if she was even luckier, seeing someone getting bent over and fucked in the alley after sneaking off to orchestrate a quick ten-dollar exchange.

Asia couldn't help but grow annoyed immediately from the disgusting sight. It was a mere eight o'clock a.m. and a bunch of niggas and dirty junkie broads were already posted around on the block, mingling amongst one another talking loudly for no reason at all. On top of that, it was brutally cold out. Icicles dangled from the rearview mirrors of the parked cars on the street, while the windows of them were coated with an icy frost.

I wish they'd get the fuck away from here. The same shit every morning, were the thoughts swirling through her head. She didn't bother to divulge those thoughts aloud however, since she didn't feel like arguing with anyone first thing in the morning. People in Philly had the tendency to get disrespectful quick; and the way her attitude was set up, things could go left just as quickly.

Even though most of the people who lived on the block were elderly, the same people still chose to loiter in front of her building since it was in the center of the street and heavily trafficked. Students and working people alike traveled the block daily in route to the bus; while drug-addicts, tricks, and hoes, quietly crept back and forth to the crime infested apartment complex across the street, in search of whatever they were craving at the time. This had been the routine since she was a young girl, growing up in the neighborhood.

Asia held her son tightly against the front of her body, his head tucked into her chest, as she did her best to protect him from the thick, gray, hazy cloud of smoke that polluted the air, and lingered in front of the building like smog. Despite holding her breath, the smoke still managed to creep into her face and tickle her nostrils. She turned her head and fought back the urge to sneeze. She despised living there, and she hated the disrespectful ass people along with it. They didn't even have the decency to move out of the way, nor did they have the decency to aid a struggling mother carrying a baby and oversized diaper bag. Just those two alone were an easy forty pounds. With their blatant lack of care, Asia wasn't surprised that they also didn't bother to put down their toxic cancer sticks and blunts. Their total disregard for a small child was unreal. But ... that's how it was in the hood.

"Aye, yo! Asia!" a familiar, masculine voice called out to her. She had moved from the front of the building and was walking down the street toward the bus stop on Chelten Avenue.

She snapped her head around in response and forced a dry smile. Trailing behind her in a big ass, bright-yellow coat was a nigga name Waleek. She had grown up with him from the neighborhood. He was a few years older than her and although she didn't know him personally, she knew *of* him. Every time he saw her, he tried to shoot his shot. For years, he had always been very blunt about the fact that he wanted her; however, she had been with Mitch, so she never gave him the time of day. Even though Mitch was now locked up, today was still no different; she didn't have time. She had to drop her son off and get to her interview.

She continued her brisk stride up the street to the bus stop. She only had a few minutes before the bus came. With thoughts of missing the bus, she sped up against the unfriendly wind that sliced viciously through the thin fabric of her North Face coat. No matter how much she did her best to stay warm, she couldn't hide the fact that she was still painfully cold.

"Where you headed?" Waleek asked, revealing his handsome grin. He reached out and gently tugged on her arm, so she could reduce her pace. She responded by pulling away. He had jogged behind her to catch up with her. It had been months since he last saw Asia, and he didn't want to let her slip past without rapping to her.

Although Waleek was very handsome, Asia silently groaned. She didn't understand why he figured she would want to stand out in the bitter, blistering cold and talk to him. She didn't give a damn how cute he was. She hated when niggas tried to holla at a chick and the elements were working against them. If it was cold, raining, or deathly hot, they needed to just let it go and try another day. These days, niggas found it convenient to holla at a chick despite the circumstances. They didn't give a damn if it was pouring down rain, and hail stones were pelting against the both of them. If she was a bad little broad, they were shooting their shot.

Asia understood their desperation though; at five-four, she was borderline stunning. Her African American and Indo-Trinidadian ethnic blend was a major factor in her exotic appearance. She had a light-brown, peanut butter skin tone, with large, expressive eyes, highlighted by thick eyelashes. With looks like hers, she stuck out like a sore thumb in that neighborhood. Even when she tried to keep it simple with no makeup and just a high ponytail, she was still undeniably beautiful. Although a few pounds overweight since the birth of her son Hasan, it didn't stop men from swooning over her daily. Mostly petite all her life, she didn't mind the weight. It had appeared to settle in all the right places, judging by the comments she regularly received.

"Waleek, I don't have time right now," Asia replied as politely as possible. Unfortunately, it still came out in somewhat of a disgruntled grumble. "I gotta catch this bus," she admitted, with discontent.

"The bus! Fuck you mean? Why ya man got you out here walking? I can give you and the young bull a ride," he offered.

It was safe for him to assume Asia was carrying a boy since Hasan was bundled up snugly in a navy-blue snowsuit. Hesitantly, she looked down at her son and contemplated that ride. The whirring wind beating against her face made her consider it. It *was* cold and she hated lugging Hasan back and forth, on and off the bus in the frigid air. However, the last time she checked, she didn't remember Waleek having a vehicle; but then again, she hadn't been in Germantown in a while.

"It's a long story Waleek," Asia said quickly, finally responding to his comment about her walking. She glanced up the street and saw the bus she needed: the twenty-six, barreling down the street. "I gotta go," she said sharply, turning off and walking away to finish the last half-dozen steps to the bus stop.

Just as Waleek went to speak, the bus pulled up and slowed to a hissing stop. Everyone at the bus stop immediately began moving so they could board. Asia turned and followed suit.

"Damn." Waleek smacked his teeth in disappointment and walked off in dismay. He'd have to catch her another time. At least he now knew that she was back in the neighborhood.

Asia watched Waleek walk further and further away, hoping he was as far away as possible by the time she attempted to board the bus with no money. It was embarrassing enough to even attempt; but what would be even more embarrassing, was if he saw her.

Turning her attention back to the bus door, Asia slipped onto the side of an elderly lady dragging a metal shopping cart filled to the brim with grocery bags. Despite the fact she smelled like a mixture of mothballs and Tide laundry detergent, Asia stayed close on her. She was hoping the lady's struggle served as a distraction and the driver didn't notice her. It was her only shot to get to the other side. If she could at least get Hasan to his grandmother's house in West Oak Lane, she could figure out the rest afterwards. She wished she at least had an old Trans Pass so she could attempt to fake swipe it. *Fuck it*, she thought. *They either gon' let me on, or they're not.*

While the lady in front of her continued struggling to pull her shopping cart up the bus's three steps, Asia followed closely behind her. Once the woman completely boarded the bus, she stopped and proceeded to dig her fare out the pocket of the long, black coat she wore. While the woman stalled, Asia figured she would use that moment to slide by her, hoping she went unnoticed. She did her best to avoid the gaze of the driver as she squeezed by with her baby and her belongings. With her head down, she held her breath and hoped for the best.

"Excuse me Miss," the driver's loud thunderous voice called out.

Asia kept heading towards the back of the bus like she didn't hear him. She quickly found a seat in the corner facing the aisle and sat down.

"Excuse me Miss!" the driver repeated.

Asia avoided looking in the front and stared straight ahead into the aisle, ignoring him.

"*You* ... with the baby, in the purple jacket!" he called out.

"He's talking to you," a scraggly, middle-aged black man said.

Asia glared at the man. She wanted to tell him to shut the fuck up. She hated when nosy people didn't mind their business. Instead of responding or cursing the man out, Asia played dumb and looked around. She looked up at the driver like she was unsure of who, or what he spoke of. She glanced around once more, still refusing to respond. That is, until he called her out.

"You!" he pointed to her. "In the purple jacket, holding the baby. You need to come up here and pay," he demanded.

"I did pay!" Asia replied firmly, her cheeks flushing hot and red from embarrassment.

"No, you didn't," he countered. "I watched you get on this bus and you didn't put any money in *or* swipe a card. Now, you need to either pay, or get up off my bus," he said like he actually owned it.

"You know what? Fuck you!" Asia snapped, hopping up. *Sorry ass nigga gon' put a bitch off the bus with her baby,* she angrily thought to herself. She hated when black people got in a funky ass position and tried to act brand new; like they couldn't do shit for anyone. He knew damn well he could have let her slide. He acted like she was cheating him personally. She was really trying to cheat Septa. All she wanted was a ride to drop off her son so she could go to her interview.

Holding her baby tightly, Asia secured her belongings over her arms, and walked swiftly to the front of the bus to exit. She didn't bother to look back. Not only was she humiliated, she couldn't help but feel angry at Mitch. Every day, she did her best to control her feelings of resentment. She hated that he'd left her and his seed out in the world, poor as fuck. She'd told him that he shouldn't be so flashy, and everybody wasn't his friend, but he didn't listen. Now look where it had him. *In jail.*

Mitch had only been getting serious paper for about a year until the robbery attempt. He spent so much that when he caught the case, he only had $80,000 in cash. With his mother handling his money, it didn't take long before that was gone. The lawyer wanted $30,000 alone just to take the case to a jury trial like Mitch wanted, despite Asia's protests.

Now here she was, out in the cold, flat broke; walking with their son. Asia's determination wouldn't let her cry, but she damn sure wanted to. She did her best not to harp on issues that were out of her control. The only thing she could do was either find a solution *or* find an alternative. Currently, she had no immediate solution to being broke. However, she did have an alternative as far as transportation.

2

―――――

"Hey, Waleek," Asia called out as she returned from the bus stop and back to the front of her building. She glanced around. Nothing had changed since she left. It was still littered with trash *and* trespassers.

Waleek had his back turned and was serving his man a small pack near the corner of the building, when he heard his name being called. Recognizing Asia's sweet voice, he looked up. A smile immediately pressed across his face. It was his lucky day. Asia was back.

"Come back when you ready for the next one," he said to the young boy he was serving. The young boy also worked for him distributing his drugs in one of his nearby drug houses. He watched the young boy walk off until he could no longer see him. After, he proceeded to stash the small, plastic bag of drugs back in his pocket. He knew it wasn't in his best interest to keep drugs on him; however, he didn't feel safe leaving them anywhere close by since the area was so heavily trafficked. He didn't want to have to damn near kill somebody for stealing from him. Retreating from the side of the building, he headed over to the front where Asia was still standing waiting patiently.

"Wassup?" he beamed; glad she had returned to rap to him.

"You think you can still give me that ride?" she asked sweetly while staring at him with her big, dreamy eyes.

She prayed he said yes, even though she had just curved him five minutes earlier. Waiting for a response, she rotated her son from one hip to the other. Hasan was getting heavier and heavier by the day. She had to get a car. There was so much she needed; she didn't know where to begin.

"No doubt," Waleek responded without hesitation.

He'd take her wherever the hell she wanted to go, if it meant a shot with her. Waleek was shallow, and when it came to looks, Asia was tough. Floyd Mayweather tough. She wasn't a hood hoe that hung out on the streets, all in nigga's faces to secure free weed and pills. She also wasn't ran through, like most of the chick's around there. The only nigga he'd ever heard of Asia dealing with was the cat from Southwest. He'd heard how Mitch rolled. He was a rising star down Southwest. If he were still home, Waleek had no doubt that he'd be one of the heavy hitters in the city. Mitch had fallen way before his time. Waleek figured just having Asia on his arm would solidify his rise in the drug game. She was the perfect chick to wife up and stunt on niggas with. Females like Asia fucked with ballin' ass niggas and that's what he was well on his way to being. The weird part was, Waleek sensed that Asia hadn't quite grasped that concept. She seemed a bit oblivious to how bad she was. She clearly had no idea how much power she could wield over dudes in the streets.

"Thank you," she said with a dimpled smile. Her brown eyes sparkled with relief. "I have an interview that's in like forty-five-minutes. I don't want to miss it," she admitted.

"I gotchu. I'll make sure you get there on time. I told you, fuck wit' me and you don't gotta worry 'bout shit," he pressed. He stared her down briefly, admiring her rare beauty. *This is a bad ass broad*, he thought to himself. He couldn't wait to see what was underneath her jacket. Something told him that she was packing some serious ass curves.

"Here. Let me take some of that shit for you," he offered with another charming smile. He reached and pulled the diaper bag off her arm and lead the way to his car that was parked about twenty feet up the block.

Asia couldn't help but notice that Waleek too, was easy on the eyes. She followed behind him and briefly admired his six-foot stature. He wore fitted denim jeans and a pair of wheat-colored Timberland field boots that looked like he had just got them straight from the shelves of Finish Line. They damn near looked clean enough to lick. Waleek carried himself well; walking with somewhat of a dip. She quickly glanced off, so he wouldn't catch her staring. He had finally stopped walking and had turned around to face her.

"This ya car?" Asia asked. Her eyebrows went up from a mixture of surprise and confusion. She glanced at him and then back to the beautiful, smoke-gray, Chevy Camaro, parked parallel against the curb. The Waleek she knew couldn't afford a car like this.

"Who's else would it be?" he laughed. "I ain't no fraudin' ass nigga. This my shit. Bought it out and out. *Cash*," he emphasized proudly.

Asia looked up at Waleek and smiled. She wasn't sure what to say. She figured he added all the extra shit in to impress her. While she liked money and appreciated men with it, she wasn't impressed with such basic materials such as a car. Besides, she had other things on her mind; she had to get to her interview. Without waiting for him to tell her, she grabbed the handle to get in, but it was locked.

"Can you unlock the door?" she asked staring at him. She was hoping he would cease the small talk and get her to where she needed to be. She didn't have a ton of time left. She was also still battling the brutal, icy gusts of wind that would religiously blow through every ten seconds.

"Oh, shit. My bad." He dug his key fob out the pocket of his oversized Helly Hansen Parka and hit the pinky-sized button on his fob.

With her free hand, Asia opened the door and sat her purse down on the seat, while Waleek came around from the opposite side of the car with her baby bag. Just as Asia was about to get in, someone yelled out.

"Ayyyee, yo! Leek! Where you going? Shit jumping!" The man threw his hands up so Waleek could spot him.

Asia recognized the man as a small-time drug dealer from the neighborhood. For Waleek, he was someone important. He was a small-time dealer that also sold his drugs.

"Hold up!" Waleek yelled in his direction. "You can go ahead and get in. I'm gon' go see what dis nigga want. I'm only gon' be a minute," he said to Asia, who was doing her best to be appreciative and stay patient.

"Okay," she said softly. Eager to escape the cold, she jumped in the passenger seat with her son. Sitting him on her lap, she closed the door and waited for Waleek to return. The smell of leather flooded her nostrils while she sat comfortably with her son shuffling around. She hadn't been in a car since Mitch was home. Anticipating an astronomical amount of legal fees, that was one of the first things chosen by his mother to go.

Waleek jogged up the street to see what his worker needed. As he headed back to the front of the building, he noticed that another one of his workers was heading in his direction. *Damn,* he thought to himself. He didn't want to keep Asia waiting but it was too much money out for him to leave. It was the second day of the month, so people still had money from the first. He watched as two separate pairs of smokers proceeded down the street from the same direction. He wasn't greedy. He was ambitious, and he was trying to get everything.

"Ay! Both y'all hold up! Stay right there. I'm not going nowhere." He turned around and walked back to his car.

"Here," he said, handing Asia the keys to his Camaro. "Go take care of what you need to take care of."

Asia took the keys and paused. "You want me to take ya car?" she asked with confusion while staring at him.

"Yeah," he laughed. "I know you can drive. I done seen you pushing whips out this bitch before. I would take you but the trap boomin' right now. I can't leave. You go 'head. Just take care of my baby."

"Th-thank you," she stuttered.

"You ain't gotta thank me. Just fuck wit' me," he said for what seemed like the hundredth time. However, Asia was starting to think that maybe she should. She opened her door and got out with Hasan.

"Fuck!" she said abruptly, just as she was stepping out. She put her hand against her head and stood there for a second with her mouth slightly agape, as if she'd suddenly forgot something. "I don't have a car seat," she remembered.

"Damn," he paused for minute. "Fuck. Alright, I gotchu," Waleek said.

Niggas just gon' have to wait. Waleek figured, if he could ease her worries and help her figure things out, then that's exactly what he was going to do. He wanted what he wanted, and Asia was going to be his by any means. He planned to do whatever it took to pull the bad, little, young broad. With her by his side, niggas were sure to envy him.

"I'll run you wherever you takin' young bull, and then you can just drop me back off and do what you need to do. And here." He reached in the left pocket of his jeans and pulled out two, crisp, one hundred-dollar bills and handed them to her.

"Go buy the lil' nigga a car seat."

"Damn ... Thank you, but you don't have to," Asia stuttered

as she reluctantly accepted the money from his extended hand. She stared at the blue bills, unsure of whether to give them back or not. Despite the fact that she needed it, she didn't want to look broke and thirsty, so she handed them back to him.

"Nah, I gotchu," he said waving her off. "Keep it. Fuck wit' me and you can get that whenever. I promise you, it's nothing," he boasted arrogantly.

Just as Asia went to speak, a car came suddenly barreling down the street, doing at least forty miles-per-hour.

"Fuck," he muttered, his expression changing from nonchalant and carefree, to alarmed.

Here this bitch come with the bullshit, were his thoughts, as his baby-mama slammed her Toyota Camry in park. He prepared himself for the scene he knew she was about to cause.

TWENTY-YEAR-OLD MALEEKA, also known as Muff, was out for blood when she got the unexpected call from her homegirl Kareema, saying she saw her baby-father Waleek on Pulaski street all up in some bitch's face. Although she dealt with other niggas from time-to-time, her and Waleek were still fucking on the regular and there was no way he was going to disrespect her in her own neighborhood, or anywhere in G-Town for that matter. He knew how she got down, so she didn't understand why he wanted to fuck with her.

After barreling down the block well above the speed limit, Muff spotted Waleek's sorry-ass leaned over, smiling on some lovey-dovey shit, with some light-skinned bitch. She couldn't believe he had the audacity to fuck with a bitch from Germantown, knowing that was her stomping grounds. She was known for her quick temper, and even more so for her notorious jealous behavior when it came to the father of her child. She had beat down so many bitches over him that he had become essentially off limits. Unfortunately, Asia hadn't been briefed.

With her daughter still strapped down in the back seat, Muff abruptly threw her car in park, causing it to jerk. Luckily, her daughter had remained sleep through the sudden stop and didn't have to witness the drama. Not that Muff gave a damn one way or another. When she got fired up, she didn't care about much of anything. Muff hopped out with her face twisted in an angry scowl. She didn't even bother to close the door behind her. "Who da fuck is that bitch Waleek?" she demanded to know as soon as she got out. Fiery blood was flowing through her veins.

"Bitch, who da fuck is you?" Muff asked Asia angrily, her face tightly balled. She immediately began screaming threats and obscenities. She clapped her hands as she spoke loudly, bouncing up and down and attracting the attention of onlookers.

"Come on Muff," Waleek groaned in response. *Not this shit again*, he thought.

"Aww, hell naw, I don't have time for this stupid shit," Asia grumbled to Waleek, who was now walking away from his car to put some distance between the two women.

Waleek already knew what to expect from Muff from being in situations like this with her before. Her behavior was predictable. If given the opportunity, she wouldn't hesitate to run up and pop off. With the space that Waleek provided, Asia immediately got out of the car with her son and scooped up her belongings. She didn't want Hasan caught up in anyone's street brawl. Asia didn't have a problem rumbling with the broad. She had been born and raised in Philly with the best of them, so she could hold her own. She just knew that she was at a disadvantage with her son on her hip. No one was worth her son's safety. However, if the bitch wanted smoke on a day that she was by herself, Asia didn't have a problem delivering it to her.

Their daughter woke up, her wails were now pronounced, yet Muff still advanced towards Waleek with aggression. Waleek shook his head in disgust at his child's mother.

"What the fuck do you want?" Waleek yelled in her face. "Get the fuck back in the car dickhead!" He pushed her back towards her vehicle. "My fuckin' daughter yellin' and shit and you out here lookin' fucking stupid! These people laughing at you!" he said, doing his best to embarrass her and persuade her to return to her vehicle.

"I don't give a fuck about these motherfuckin' people," she spat, snatching away from him angrily. She glared around at the people looking at her and rolled her eyes.

"Why da fuck is you out here in bitches faces! Tell me dat!" She swung her hands erratically like she'd come prepared to fight.

She glanced at Asia and the sight of her made her even angrier. Muff couldn't deny the fact that the chick was beautiful. Something told her that this chick was going to be a problem. Not only was she attractive, her face lacked what Muff saw in most bitches that she confronted: fear. She watched Asia's face remain emotionless while she walked off down the street.

"Don't run bitch!" Muff called out. However, Asia didn't bother to respond. She continued to scurry up the street as quickly as she could to escape the drama.

"Yo, Asia!" Waleek called out to her desperately, without thinking. He hadn't gotten her contact information or anything. *This stupid ass bitch stays fuckin' shit up for me*, Waleek thought to himself.

Seeing Waleek's disregard for her own feelings caused Muff's already budding anger to go from warm ... to scorching.

"What you worried 'bout that bitch for!" she screamed.

With fury, she drew her arm back and charged Waleek, swinging with as much strength as she could muster. Waleek's sharp reflexes allowed him to dodge the hits; however, Muff kept them coming until one of them connected with his mouth, driving his lip into his teeth.

"Bitch chill da fuck out!" he screamed angrily.

He grabbed her with so much strength, he nearly lifted her off her feet. *I ought to break your fuckin' neck out here*, he thought, holding her tightly by the thin material of her dress. It never failed; Muff knew exactly when and where to show her ass. Had they been alone in a room, he would have drove her head into a wall for hitting him in the mouth like that. He felt a tinge of blood on his tongue and determined she'd busted his lip. He quickly ran his tongue over the bruise, feeling the indentation his teeth had left. He could also feel the skin hanging loosely from it.

While he loved his baby-mother dearly, it was jealous, irrational antics like this that caused him to see other people. The bitch had no morals or principles. His daughter was in the backseat, now screaming at the top of her three-year-old lungs from all the noise her mother was making. Muff hadn't even bothered to shut the car door or turn off the engine. Not only could their daughter hear the domestic dispute, she could also see it.

Still holding Muff tightly, he glared down at her in repulse. Albeit pretty, Waleek didn't like what he saw. Muff was a hood-chick to the core. She partied, hustled niggas, and stayed in some bullshit. This was what her life consisted of: being ratchet and chasing behind him like the typical hood-rat baby mother, determined to make the father's life a living hell.

Dressed in typical hood-rat attire, Muff had come in an all-black cotton dress and a pair of Timberlands in the same color. In the dead of winter, she wore no coat, jacket, or tights; her exposed skin cold to the touch. She looked like she'd come strictly prepared for a fight. Her behavior was sad, since Muff was a very pretty girl; although one wouldn't be able to tell since she kept twenty inches of weave in her head and had three inches of thick, black eyelashes extending off her face. Ghetto fabulous was probably the best way to describe her. All the nigga's in the hood wanted her, except of course, the one that mattered.

3

———————

Asia was sprawled out on the faded, floral-patterned couch when she heard light tapping at the door. She figured it was someone for her mother since she wasn't expecting any company. She didn't feel like getting up and telling them that her mother wasn't there, so she sat still. Her mother Sheila had left out with her little brother to pick up a few things from the market. The same market that she had an interview scheduled at but never made.

Asia glanced at the door, but eventually redirected her gaze back to the tv she was watching, still unwilling to get out of her comfortable position. Part of the reason was, she didn't want to accidentally wake Hasan, who was sprawled out and lying on his back on the opposite end of the couch. She looked to the opposite end where he laid. She had one foot jammed on the side of him in the cracks of the couch, while the other was on the opposite side of him. He was snoring softly, his eyes closed tight and his mouth slightly agape.

After ignoring the visitor another minute or so, the taps at the door returned. *The fuck,* she thought. With a grunt, she rose from the couch, being careful to lift her legs over her son so as not to kick or wake him. She grabbed the remote from off the coffee table and hit the pause button on the DVD player. They didn't have cable, so she was re-watching one of her favorite movies: Baby Boy.

Walking to the door, she didn't bother to ask who it was. She didn't want to risk waking Hasan. After being back and forth in the bitter cold air the past couple of days, he was coming down with a nasty cough and a runny nose. He had been fussy for most of the day. After giving him a small plunger of medicine, he had finally dozed off, giving her a well-deserved break.

Glancing through the peep hole, she smacked her teeth and rolled her eyes. *What the fuck this nigga want*, she thought to herself. Some nerve he had, after the drama from earlier. She turned the gold knob on the deadbolt as well as the small lock on the handle of the door, so she could open it.

"What?" she asked Waleek with an attitude. She didn't even open the door fully. Only half her body was visible, while her head was angled to the side to indicate she didn't have time, nor a desire to hear what he had to say.

"Can I talk to you for a minute?" he asked, his wide, brown eyes, seemingly piercing through her. Something about the way he looked at her felt like she was being undressed.

"Say what you gotta say," she mumbled, while rolling her eyes.

"I just came to say I was sorry. Man, I didn't know my baby-mom was gon' pull up like that."

"Of course, you didn't," Asia said sarcastically. She still stood partly shielded by the door. She clutched the side. She had a strong desire to shut it in his face.

"I didn't!" he said, his voice increasing.

"Keep ya voice down. If you wake my son ..." she threatened.

"My bad. Look ... What can I do to make it up to you?" he

asked, cutting to the chase.

"Make it up to me?" she scoffed. "Nigga I had a fucking interview. Fuckin' around with you and ya stupid ass baby-mother, I didn't even make that shit."

She didn't bother disclosing the fact that she had no money to begin with. She probably would have never made it anyway.

"Well how 'bout this?" he began, reaching down in his pocket and pulling out a thick wad of money with a thick tan rubber band wrapped around it to hold it neatly in place.

"How much was the job gon' pay you?" he asked.

"I don't know," she shrugged, curious to see what he was hinting at. "It was Shoprite. Probably minimum wage," she said.

"Okay, so what's that, seven dollars and twenty-five cents? So, like $300 a week." He pulled the rubber band off his knot and began snatching hundred dollar bills off from it.

"Here," he said, handing her ten bills. "That's a stack. Ya pay for a month."

Asia looked at Waleek's extended hand and took the money from it. She couldn't help but allow a smile to creep onto her face and remove the frown she had previously been wearing.

"Thank you Waleek," she said. He had no idea how much she could use the money.

"I'm here to help," he said with a smile.

Immediately, her annoyance with him became curiosity. What did he really want from her? What did he see in her that had him so persistent? Asia looked at him and couldn't help but finally appreciate how attractive he really was. Waleek was extremely handsome; his skin bathed in an expresso colored hue. He had the brightest white teeth and the cutest smile. Although Philly men were notorious for their big, long beards, Waleek chose to wear his short and tapered neatly against his face.

"I appreciate it," she said, catching herself staring.

"You gon' be mine," he said with confidence. He glared at

her and grinned boyishly.

"We'll see," she said. For the first time, she wasn't so confident in her response.

"Na, you'll see," he assured her. "I'm gon' come get you tomorrow. You and young bull. We can go sit down and eat or something. Somewhere out in the county or something," he said. He planned to play it safe until they became official. As soon as they did, he was going to get Muff in line.

"Okay, I'm wit' it," Asia said. She went to say something else but hearing Hasan's soft cries stopped her. "My son up. Hold on," she said abruptly. She walked off to check on him and make sure he was ok. Waking up and not seeing anyone around, had alarmed him.

"Hey boy," she said soothingly to Hasan who was in mid-whine with his eyes darting around the living room in search of her. She picked him up and gently pat his back to comfort him.

"My boy woke up," she said proudly to no one in particular, as she returned to the door to see Waleek off.

"Yeah, I see. You gon spoil him. He a big boy. He can cry a little. Right man!" he said to Hasan. Hasan looked at him and frowned. He had no idea who the man in front of him was and decided he wasn't going to be friendly. Waleek laughed. *You gon' get used to me lil nigga*, he thought.

"Look. I'm gon' let you go. Give me yo' number so I can hit you up later."

Asia proceeded to ramble off her number while Waleek punched it in his phone to store it.

"I'mma hit you in a bit so you can lock my shit in," he said as he walked off backward.

Asia closed the door and sat back down, while Waleek headed back to the streets.

He was about to pull an all-nighter. He had just given Asia a grand, on top of the two hundred he had given her earlier. If that didn't win her over, then he didn't know what would. He wasn't concerned about the money. It was the beginning of the month where he could easily make $10,000 a day thanks to the cluster of abandoned houses nearby. Using those spots as a place to distribute his drugs was making him a fortune. Additionally, he allowed the users to get high right there in the same spot. That way, they would keep coming back. The worst thing for a smoker was to buy drugs and then have to try and figure out where you were going to use them at. It was a win-win situation for him.

The riskiest part of his organization was delivering the drugs to his workers and then transporting and selling them back at the house. So far, so good. The houses were in the cut, all by their lonesome at the end of a dark block. Through word of mouth, it was quickly becoming the place to be. Waleek's thoughts quickly shifted back to Asia. He had just recently become plugged in. He was going to be king, and she was going to be his queen.

LATER THAT EVENING, Asia sat in her room trying to get her son to sleep. As usual, Hasan squirmed, cried, and rubbed his tiny eyes in frustration as he desperately fought sleep. *Go the fuck to sleep*, she thought as she stared at her stubborn son. Asia sighed but continued to gently tap his back to comfort him. His routine was the same every night. He would never just go to sleep; he always chose to fight it instead. It didn't make much sense to her. Asia reached down and adjusted his soft, powder blue blanket. She made sure it was pulled up comfortably around his neck. For five minutes, she watched as Hasan's eyes fluttered constantly, until they settled and became still. *Bout time*, she thought to herself, finally breathing a sigh of relief. He kept her running all day. She was worn out and the only thing she wanted to do was grab her nightclothes and go take a long shower. Hasan stayed glued to her hip, so when he went down for naps or finally fell asleep for the night, she took advantage of the precious alone time.

Just as she went to stand, a sudden burst of thunderous laughter traveled throughout the house. Hasan's eyes immediately flew open. *Fuck!* Asia thought. Hasan immediately started to sob and whine from being forced out of his sleep. Springing to her feet in frustration, Asia snatched her phone off her dresser to look at the time. It was eleven o'clock p.m. Temporarily ignoring her son's cries, Asia snatched open her door and marched into the living room where her mother was sitting with her Aunt Betty that lived up the street, and a guy name Lou from the neighborhood. They were at the card table her mother kept folded up in the closet. Asia didn't know why she even bothered to put it up, since she seemed to pull it out every day. Day or night, her mother always had company over, either playing cards or sitting around drinking beer. Cooking, hanging out, and drinking beer had been her routine since she started collecting a check for her little brother Jalil. Along with all the assistance she received, the little SSI check provided Sheila a comfortable life in the hood doing absolutely, fucking nothing.

"Ma, can y'all please keep it down? Hasan's trying to sleep," she said. She did her best to be respectful considering she was addressing her elder and it wasn't her house; however, no one could mistake the hostility in her voice that she did her best to mask.

Sheila looked to her daughter like she'd lost her mind. Her broke ass didn't pay one bill in the house to be making any requests. "Excuse me?" she questioned her daughter, her eyes narrowing and brows wrinkling. Sheila brought her half-smoked Newport to her lips and pulled from the butt, leaving behind an imprint from the bright-red lipstick that coated them. She inhaled and exhaled a cloud of smoke that lingered around the table. She glanced back over at her daughter, so she could proceed.

"Can you please ask them to keep it down?" Asia whined. However, this time, her tone and volume were a bit lower.

"Who the fuck is loud?" Sheila questioned. She rolled her eyes, picked through the hand of cards she was holding up and then laid one down on the table. "We barely saying shit," she said, blowing out another breath of smoke.

"Ma, I'm not trying to be smart, but they're loud. I heard Mr. Lou's voice way in my room with the door closed. I laid Hasan down at eight-o-clock, and he's woken up four or five ti—"

"Get the fuck out my face, Asia!" her mother screamed. "Now, I'm being loud bitch! You don't pay shit in here for you to be coming asking somebody to keep it the fuck down!"

She knew that response was coming. Asia spun around on her heels and stormed out of the living room. Her mother was always trying to show off for her raggedy ass company.

"I hate this fucking house!" she unexpectedly blurted out. Asia didn't mean to say it aloud but somehow it managed to slip out. Loud enough for her mother to hear.

"What you say?" her mother yelled out from the living room.

Sheila mashed out her half-smoked cigarette in the glass ashtray that was sitting in the middle of the card table. Resting it gently on the side, she pushed herself back in her folding chair and got up.

"Sheila will you leave that child alone, please?" her sister Betty said. She knew Sheila all too well. She had Satan's temper and once she got started, there was no stopping her.

"Fuck that. She always talkin' shit. Bitch don't pay nothing and want somebody to cater to what the fuck she wants."

Betty shook her head and sat down the row of cards she was holding. She watched as Sheila proceeded to march into the back to fuck with Asia anyway.

"What da fuck you say Asia!" Sheila asked, opening, and entering Asia's room.

"Mom please," Asia groaned. "I'm trying to get Hasan to sleep. I'm not 'bout to go back and forth wit' you."

Asia looked at her mother in frustration. She definitely wasn't the typical grandmother. She was selfish and didn't give a damn about nobody but herself. Asia rolled her eyes to the side and continued staring at the wall to avoid eye-contact with her mother. She unsuccessfully rocked her son in her arms. He was now wide awake. His big, bright eyes wandering around the room and ultimately turning their focus to his irate grandmother.

"I don't give a damn what you tryin' to do! This my mother-fuckin' house!" she reminded her. Her lip was curled up and perspiration was now dotting the front of her head. Asia had fired her up. But then again, it didn't take much. Sheila had grown up being taught that disrespecting your elders got your ass beat, and Asia's grown ass was no exception.

"Learn to watch your fuckin' mouth! Especially when you' laying your broke, funky ass under someone else's roof!" Sheila picked her orange lighter up from off the table and proceeded to re-light the cigarette she had just put out a minute ago.

"You can get the fuck out," Sheila continued to mumble as she sparked her lighter to the bent cigarette that now dangled from the corner of her lips. "You and that little, nappy-headed ass baby," she added for insult.

Asia shook her head and grit her teeth so hard, she thought they would fall the fuck out. She did her best to control the anger that was flowing through her body. She looked at her mother with hate and disgust. Since she could remember, Sheila had been a mean, shitty ass mother. One of those mothers that all your friends hated. Since Asia was fifteen, she had been working; and not because she wanted to. She worked because she *had* to. As a child, she and her little brother had the bare minimum. While they were properly fed because of the government's food stamp program, they didn't have all the extra little luxuries the other kids had. If they were lucky, they got two pair of shoes per year. One at tax time, when their mother let someone carry them on their taxes and maybe a pair when school started. They wore hand-me-down clothes year-round and never went anywhere. McDonald's, Chuckie Cheese, skating; shit that normal kids would do every now and then, they never did.

As soon as Asia became old enough to work, she went and got a job. Once she got a few dollars in her pocket and was able to do things for herself, her treatment from her mother became even worse. According to Sheila, Asia thought she was the shit because she had her hair done. Asia thought she was better than everybody because she had a few *funky ass dollars*. It also didn't help that as soon as she did have a few extra dollars, her little brother Jalil began stealing. With her entire household seemingly against her desire to better herself, Asia began saving money to get as far away from them as possible. Once she met Mitch, she was able to do just that. Asia didn't bother responding to her mother's antics. She wished she had somewhere else to go. If she had other options, she would have left.

"You ain't got shit to say now, huh?" Sheila muttered as she stood in the door, her lip still curled up into an ugly scowl. She glared at Asia, who was sitting down next to Hasan and patting his back to get him back to sleep. She still didn't respond, so Sheila rolled her eyes, muttered some undetectable curse words, and walked off.

Asia rolled her eyes, then got up to shut her door. Before she could sit back down on her bed and continue to try getting Hasan back to sleep, loud music began hammering through the house. R. Kelly's soulful voice began to blare through the house so loudly, Asia could feel the walls vibrate.

Fuck this shit! I can't take another minute of this shit! Asia thought angrily. If she were a ghetto bitch that didn't give a damn, she would beat her mother's ass. However, she refused to disrespect her that way; yet, she too, refused to continue to be disrespected. Asia wasn't asking for much; she wasn't asking to be catered to. All she wanted was for them to keep it down so Hasan could get a little sleep. What grandmother wouldn't want that as well?

Asia jumped up from her spot on the bed and began furiously grabbing her things. She didn't have much, but she figured she was going to take as much as she could. If she didn't, she knew it was going to be missing by the time she returned for it. She grabbed Hasan's diaper bag and began stuffing it. She also grabbed her travel bag from the corner of the small room and began stuffing it with a few items she had snatched down from the clothing rack in her room. Pants, shirts, onesies, socks, and sleepers; she grabbed as much as she could take in the two bags. She was getting the fuck out of her mother's house. If someone wasn't stealing from her, she was being disrespected. Enough was enough! She vowed she'd never come back here to stay again. She didn't care if she had to sell pussy; she wasn't returning to this shit hole.

Asia grabbed her phone from off the bed. She was about to call an uber but then decided to call Waleek instead.

Can you come get me please? My mom trippin' and I gotta get the fuck out of here.

He immediately replied, *Yeah, I gotchu.* Waleek didn't ask any questions. He figured whatever was going on, could be an advantage for him.

Asia dug through her purse and made sure she still had the $1,200 Waleek had given her earlier. She knew she did, since she had the bag glued to her side since she'd received it. However, she didn't want to take any chances. She needed it for what she was about to do next.

4
____

Asia tossed her two bags into the backseat of Waleek's car. She climbed into the front seat, shut the door, and then proceeded to strap herself in with Hasan on her lap. He babbled to himself and quietly played with his hands, completely oblivious to the fact that he was now homeless.

Waleek glanced over at her. He didn't want to pry but he needed to know at least a little about what was going on. He could tell by the solemn look on her face that something was wrong. He knew she wouldn't have drug her baby out into the bitter cold at night if there wasn't something up.

"You okay?" he asked with concern. He could see anger, as well as a little bit of sadness on her young face. Her eyes were damp, and her nose had just a touch of redness at the tip. She had been crying.

"Yeah, I'm okay," she responded. She held her son tightly as he continued to play to himself quietly. Asia looked at Waleek sadly. "I can't stay there," she said, her voice cracking as she fought back sobs. She took a deep breath, and then swallowed the hard lump in her throat to suppress the cries dying to escape.

"What happened?" he asked.

Asia proceeded to tell him what went down. She clenched her teeth in frustration and paused frequently. She was already frustrated by the fact that she didn't have shit, but it hurt her even worse that she had to subject herself to her mother's treatment out of desperation. Sheila constantly made it clear that she didn't fuck with Asia, now it was also clear that she didn't fuck with her only grandson either. Asia continued to fight back the desire to cry. She didn't want Waleek to see her cry. She didn't want to be viewed as weak. Her pride wouldn't allow it.

Waleek provided his undivided attention and listened intently. When Asia was done, he finally decided to speak. "I told you I got you. Don't stress yaself over that shit. Fuck wit' me and you good," he said. He extended his hand out and touched her chin to reassure her. An unsure smile surfaced on her face.

Waleek looked down at Hasan. "I got both of y'all," he assured her. Unbothered, Hasan began to stir around quietly in Asia's lap.

"Now ... The first thing we gotta do, is figure out where y'all gon stay tonight." To Waleek, her problems were miniscule. To his luck, he knew he could easily help her.

"Well, I still got the money you gave me earlier. I figured that could pay for my room." She sighed and paused for a second. "At least a few weeks ... and then, I'll figure out what to do from there."

Waleek let out a chuckle. "A few weeks where? At the Red Roof Inn?" he asked. He hadn't given her much, so that money wasn't going far.

"You not staying there. They probably got bugs and shit. I ain't getting' bit up, and neither are y'all."

Asia looked at him, and this time, the smile that appeared on her face was genuine. Waleek made it clear that he cared and that he was going to look out for them. For the first time since Mitch had been gone, Asia felt a little more at peace. She felt like she really didn't have to worry about anything. Something told her that Waleek was going to take care of them.

"Nah, y'all not going there," he reiterated with finality. He started up his car and the engine roared to life.

"So, where are we going? Well better yet ... Where do *you* think I should stay?" she asked with emphasis.

"Chill," he laughed. *Let me handle this shit, ma,* he thought to himself. "I told you I got you. I'm gon' take y'all somewhere nice."

Asia didn't bother to respond. She held her son and sat back in her seat. She would now let Waleek lead. A part of her felt like that was for the best. It felt good to have a nigga back in her corner.

"I need a one-bedroom. And I also need a crib if you got one," Waleek said to the smiling, blond-haired receptionist that was at the front desk of the hotel. When Waleek left Germantown to find Asia a place to stay, he knew he wanted her to be somewhere comfortable, especially since he didn't know how long she was going to be staying there. He had stayed at the Windsor Suites in Philadelphia years ago and knew this would be the perfect place for Asia and her baby, until he helped her get situated and into a crib.

"That's not a problem," the receptionist said with a pearly-white smile. She proceeded to search through her computer system to find an available suite. As he stood there waiting patiently, Waleek glanced at the gold-plated nametag pinned to her shirt. Her name was Megan.

"I do have a one-bedroom available. The crib is going to be an extra five-dollars per day," she said for informational purposes only. She doubted the man in front of her would complain about an extra five dollars per day, especially since he didn't appear to be experiencing any financial hardship. He'd pulled up in a new sports car that he'd boldly parked on the sidewalk, directly in front of the hotel's entrance.

"How much?" Waleek asked.

"Right now, the rate is $148 a day. How long did you need it?" She looked up at him and waited for him to respond.

"Two weeks," he replied. Waleek figured; Asia would need at least that. He was confident she could find a job in two weeks, and within a month, she would be out of there.

"Okay!" Megan responded with another beaming, bright smile. She'd initially assumed he would only ask for a night. Most of the young, black guys that came in were only interested on getting in and out. She was more than happy to rent him a room for that time frame. She was eager to get her sales up. She hadn't been working there very long and she wanted to prove that she was just as productive as the other receptionists who'd been there longer. After selecting a few tabs on her computer screen, she proceeded to search thoroughly, making sure she chose the best one-bedroom she could find, she had him all set.

"So, it's going to be $2,196 with tax," she said. She waited patiently for him to pay.

"Damn!" he laughed. "That's high as fuck," he said. He would be lying if he said he wasn't expecting it to be. He dug in his pants pocket, pulled out a fat wad of money that was neatly wrapped in a thick, tan rubber band, and proceeded to count out $2,200.

"Here you go," he said after he was done counting. He rewrapped his money and stuffed the wad back in his pocket while the receptionist proceeded to recount the money. After ensuring that the count was accurate, she told Waleek to wait,

so she could deposit the money into the hotels safe that sat
tucked away in the office. He waited quietly while she was gone
for what seemed like five minutes. He looked around the lobby
and admired the scene. Located in Center City, it was impeccably clean with modern fixtures throughout. The sounds of a
rippling water and the hum of a filter drew him to the beautiful
fountain smack dab in the middle of the lobby. It was
surrounded with lush green vegetation and had sparkling blue
water that was lit up with an array of colorful lights. The patter
of Megan's footsteps brought his attention back to the desk in
front of him.

"Alright! You're just about set!" she said, returning back to
her spot at her computer.

She pulled out a plastic door key from off her desk and acti-
vated it so he and his party could access the room. "You're going
to be on the second floor. When you get off the elevator, you're
going to make a right."

She leaned over the desk and handed him the key that was
neatly tucked in a brochure.

"So, the pool is open every day from ten o'clock a.m. to ten
o'clock p.m. We serve an American continental breakfast every
day from five to ten in the morning and there is no wi-fi
passcode."

Waleek listened as she continued to ramble off what ameni-
ties were available. When she was done, he quickly bopped
back out to the car, where he found Asia and Hasan drifted off
to sleep. After finding a parking spot he woke them up and they
headed to the suite he'd reserved. When he opened the door to
the room, Asia was taken aback by how nice the place was. She
quickly scanned the place, looking around like she was a little
kid in the toy store for the very first time.

"This is nice," she gushed. "You didn't have to do all this."
She stopped and just stared at Waleek.

"I know. But I want to. I fuck with you. I want to make sure you good. Better yet, let me rephrase that. I'm *going* to make sure you're good," he said.

"Thank you she said." She redirected her gaze from Waleek and went over and sat down on the couch. She noticed the crib in the corner of the living room.

"You asked them for a crib?" she asked with a smile creeping up on her face.

"Yeah," Waleek responded without hesitation. He didn't think anything of it. Since Hasan appeared only about a year old, he naturally assumed that he would need a crib. He would have done the same thing for his own daughter at that age.

Although the gesture didn't mean much to him, to Asia, it was a grand gesture.

"Thanks again, Waleek. Oh!" She laid her son down on the couch and rummaged through her purse. "I still have the money you gave me earlier." She unzipped the side pocket of her purse and dug out the cash. Extending her arm, she handed him the cash. "Here."

A wide grin formed on Waleek's handsome, chocolate face. "What's this?" he asked, looking down to the cash in her hand without accepting it. "That's yours. Anything that I give you, belongs to you. I'll never take anything back that I gave you. And I'll never let you pay for something I can afford. Put your money back in your purse. I paid the room up for two weeks. As long as you're wit' me, nobody gon' ever put you out of shit again."

Waleek leaned down and unexpectedly gave Asia a kiss on her forehead. The sudden act of affection took her by surprise. Waleek was so hood but it was clear that he was feeling her. She looked up to him with lusty eyes and smiled sweetly.

"Thanks again for everything." She didn't know how she could repay him. But then again ... she had an idea.

Asia's heavy eyes fluttered lightly back open. She looked around and had to remind herself where she was and how she got there. After a few seconds, she realized she had dozed off on the couch of the hotel with Hasan on her chest. He too was fast asleep, his tiny baby breaths causing his little back to rise and fall. Asia let out a deep yawn. With a heavy body, she scooted herself up off the couch, pushed her body up and walked through the room with her son. She gently placed him down in the crib nearby and then covered him up with one of his little blankets she had packed in his diaper bag.

Asia still couldn't believe that Waleek had asked for it. The simple fact that he thought of her son, moved her. She walked into the small, but fully equipped kitchen nearby. She had a little electric stove, a sink, and even ample counter space to prepare meals. She opened a random cabinet above the sink and saw a pair of dishes. There was also a utensil holder that had a set of spoons, forks, and everything you needed to prepare meals comfortably. She glanced at the microwave. It was two o'clock a.m. She shook her head solemnly and made a vow to get Hasan on a schedule immediately.

Asia leaned back casually against the counter and looked around. She was still struggling to take everything in. She really had left her mom's again. This time however, she knew that she would probably never be welcome again. Her mother was petty. She would rather allow Asia to struggle on the street rather than assist her. For Sheila, it was the simple fact that she felt Asia disrespected her and felt she was holier than thou. Sheila couldn't grasp that *better than everyone* attitude she thought Asia had since she didn't have shit to or in her name for that matter.

As soon as Asia walked out that door with that little $1,200, she knew that she was going to have no choice but to step it up. She either had to grind or she had to hustle. She knew Waleek liked her. He had gone out of his way to show her that. She knew that being his girl was going to be her hustle to make sure she, nor her son wanted for shit. She planned to get a job but fucking with Waleek was going to get her on her feet and back to being the bitch she was when Mitch was home. Asia knew she was a bad bitch; however, she did her best not to use her looks and personality to manipulate men. As the struggle to get on her feet, and raise her son became more pronounced, she knew she was being a damn fool. She knew that *she* was her best asset, and she intended to use it to accumulate as much as possible. She was tired of struggling. The only direction now, was up ... and to the top she planned to go.

5

A sia stepped out of the shower with her skin still dripping beads of water to the floor. She gently pulled out a towel that sat nestled above the toilet and between two steel metal bars. As she patted her skin dry with it, she couldn't help but appreciate the sound she heard. Except for the occasional tap and drip of water from the shower head, she heard nothing. Silence. She smiled. Although she was naturally a little worried, she was confident that things would work out for the best. She was confident that she had made the right decision. No matter what, she wasn't going to dwell on it. *What's done is done*, she thought to herself.

Asia finished drying off and went to peek at her son in the living room. He was still on his back, sprawled out and sleeping soundly. *That's all my baby needed*, she thought. *Just some peace and quiet.* Out of instinct and habit, she checked the front door of the suite and made sure the door was locked. She set the deadbolt in place and headed back to the room so she could lay down. She glanced around the suite and finally realized how comfortable it was, as well as how nice it looked. Waleek had done a good job choosing a spot. The suite itself was very clean with contemporary furniture pieces. Smack dab in the middle of the suite was a tan couch, accompanied by two dark blue accent chairs that sat diagonally across. What made the room décor pop, was the pillows that accented the both. The pillows were both plush and multi-colored making the room bright, while still providing the cozy and warm feeling. It was literally a mini apartment, with a living room, bedroom, small kitchen, and full bathroom.

Asia left on the light in the living room so Hasan wouldn't go nuts if he woke up in the dark. He wasn't a fan of the dark and would wake up and raise holy hell if he found himself alone in it. She walked into the bedroom at the back of the suite and was surprised when she saw Waleek sprawled out on the bed. She hadn't heard him come in. They had never actually agreed that he would be staying the night but the more she gazed at him, the more she wouldn't mind if he stayed. As Waleek lay quietly, she couldn't help but continue admiring his physique. He had removed his shirt and pants, and now lay on the bed in a pair of bright red, Ethika boxers. His boots, pants, shirt, and shiny, gold jewelry were neatly placed on the mahogany-colored, wooden desk near the door.

Asia took a minute and just stared at him quietly. She had to admit; he was fine as fuck. His body was tight and nothing short of perfection. His smooth, dark chocolate skin looked as if it had been kissed by the sun a thousand times. He was lean and long. His legs toned and calf muscles taut. For the first time in a long time, Asia felt her body warm up and seem to come alive. She felt her pussy flowing wet with juices. She reached down and touched in between her legs to see if it was as wet as it felt. It was. It felt slippery and moist to the touch. She pulled her hand from her center and rubbed her thumb and index finger together.

Allowing her towel to slip down to the floor, Asia walked over and climbed up on, and into the bed to lay by Waleek.

Feeling movement, followed by a humanly presence, he woke up. It was dark, but he could feel Asia's soft mango-scented skin brush against him. Asia's touch gave him goosebumps all over his body. He immediately felt his pole stiffen up.

"Bout time you laid ya ass down," he mumbled in a low voice. He slung his hand over her midsection and pulled her closer to him. She smelled so good and he just had to have her right up under him.

"I had to put Hasan to sleep and take a shower," she responded. Asia took a deep breath. She could feel Waleek's stiff dick pressing up against her back. She couldn't lie; feeling that shit against her had her heart racing. She wondered how it would feel stuffed inside of her. She also wondered if he knew how to use it. As ghetto and fine as he was, he'd better. Asia hadn't had such wicked thoughts in a long time. She didn't understand how bitches could be flat broke and worried about fucking and sucking dick. Now that she laid beside Waleek, she knew her financial situation would drastically improve. She could now indulge a little.

"I just want to say thank you again," she said quietly. She stared in the direction of the wall. She couldn't see anything, but her thoughts playing out in her mind.

"I told you I got you," he said. Asia didn't respond. She used her hand to gently stroke the arm Waleek had wrapped around her.

Feeling her soft hands glide against his skin gave Waleek tingles, in addition to the goosebumps he already had. Every fiber and cell in his body became alert and hyper-sensitive. That simple touch caused her to smell a little sweeter; made her skin feel a little softer; and caused his dick to feel a little harder. He yearned to be inside of her. He had to have her. He didn't want to rush her or pressure her, but thinking with his dick, led him to make his move.

Waleek leaned in and used his full lips to kiss her gently on the neck. The heat he emitted when he knelt in front of her, made her feel as though she was melting inside. If she had on panties, the anticipation would have caused her to cream them. So much, that it caused her to moan gently. As soon as Waleek heard it, he knew he had her.

He kissed and nuzzled up against her collar once more, but this time he used his tongue to trail a path from the nape of her neck to her earlobe. He felt Asia's body tense up. However, he felt her relax when he took his hand and slipped it in between her thighs. As he used his hands to part her swollen pussy lips, he could feel her sticky nectar coating the insides of her thighs. He wondered how it tasted. Waleek rose from the spot he was laying in and quickly pushed down his boxers. Before Asia could change her mind, he climbed on top of her, parted her legs wide, dropped to his belly and buried his face in her sweet box. It tasted just as good as he thought it would. As she squirmed and gripped her thighs against his shoulders, he went to work indulging in the sugary goodness of her pussy. He thrust his tongue in and out of her pussy hole while occasionally using his warm, wet lips to lick, suck, kiss and pull on her clit.

Asia moaned from the intense euphoric feeling Waleek's mouth gave her. It felt as if he was reintroducing her body to a whole new world. A whole new feeling. As he flicked and swirled his tongue up, down, and around her pussy, she felt her body weaken and seemingly cave into the king-size mattress.

"Mmmmmm ... Yesssss Daddyyy," she purred, finally giving in to the overwhelming act. She didn't give a fuck how she sounded. She couldn't help it. The nigga was talented, and it felt way too good to suppress her satisfaction. *Where the fuck have you been*, she thought to herself. If she knew Waleek had a mouth like that, she would have been fucked with him. His head game was superb.

Hearing Asia's moans and comments caused Waleek's dick

to go from hard, to concrete. He wanted to turn her little ass out; eat her pussy so good, she'd never leave. Showing off his skills, Waleek flattened his tongue against her pussy and took long swipes up and down her treasure like he was licking a popsicle.

"Fuckkkkk," Asia growled. She clenched her teeth and grabbed the pillow beside her so she could moan into it. She didn't want to wake Hasan up.

"Mmmmmm Daddy! Eat this pussy," she moaned desperately. She didn't want him to stop, but part of her felt like he was taking away all her willpower. All her reasoning skills. With a tongue and mouth like his, she knew that she would easily be a damn fool for him.

Waleek gripped her thighs firmly and pulled her down closer to his face so she couldn't run. He felt Asia squirm and try to pull back to get away. He continued to suck on her pussy furiously. His chin was wet, and her sweet fluids trickled down off his mouth and all over the bed. Asia was literally laying in a pool of her own juices. Just as she nearly reached her peak, Waleek snatched his mouth away, hopped up, and thrust his nine-inch dick inside of her. When he entered her, Asia felt like her soul had left her body, and for a second ... she thought she had died and gone to heaven. Waleek hadn't even stroked twice, and she was cumming violently all over his dick. She dug her fingers into his back and wrapped her legs around his torso.

"Ohhh my fucking gawd!" she panted. "I'm coming!" she said.

Hearing those words was like music to Waleek's ears. Asia had the best pussy he had ever had. It was so warm and tight, and so fucking wet. He thrust his dick deeply, in and out of her tight wet canal, her sugary walls gripping him. She felt so good to him; he couldn't contain himself.

"Damnnnn," he cried out "You got some good ass pussy," he admitted. *You definitely mine now,* he thought to himself

A few more thrusts and Waleek couldn't last any longer. He quickly snatched his wet dick out of Asia and gripped it tightly while he bust a hot load in the palm of his hand.

"Fuck!" he groaned. His forehead coated with perspiration, he collapsed beside her, still clutching a fistful of semen. After a few minutes, he got up and went to wash his hands. When he returned, he cuddled next to Asia and threw his arm around her.

Asia lay on her back and stared at the dark ceiling. Her body was still tingling from the intense orgasm she had just had. She let a soft smile creep along her face, as Waleek scooted her body closer to her.

"I gotta go clean up," she said softly. She was still moist from not only their combination of juices, but the powerful ass orgasm she had just had. She was still doing her best to recover from it. Waleek removed his arm so she could get up. He couldn't deny the fact that he was feeling her. She wasn't like most girls that he just fucked and ducked. He really liked Asia. She was beautiful and she had some bomb-ass pussy. He knew that he would easily grow to love her. As she scooted out the bed and stepped down onto the floor, he studied her. Before she walked out the room she turned and stared at him. She thought he was sleep. A smile spread across her face while she stared at him. He knew he had her.

6

THREE MONTHS LATER

Asia strapped Hasan in his car seat and pushed the door shut so they could head out. She opened the driver side door and hopped in the front seat. "You ready to go see Da-Da," she said to Hasan, mimicking a baby voice similar to his own. She looked back at her son and he was smiling brightly and looking out the back window. She wished she could be as carefree as he always appeared to be.

Asia started up her car and adjusted the seat so she could be closer to the steering wheel. *Why the fuck this nigga got the seat so far back*, she thought to herself. Waleek liked to use her car every now and then to switch things up. With him being a well-known hustler in Germantown, he had to. He didn't want to be too predictable. After adjusting her seat, Asia hooked up her phone to the car's Bluetooth. Her and Hasan were about to embark on a nearly three-hour ride, so she had to get her music right before they left. It had been damn near six-months since she'd last seen Mitch, but that was about to change today. A lot had changed.

Since Waleek had come into her life, things had improved dramatically. For starters, she no longer caught the bus. Waleek had put some money to the side and surprised her with a cocaine-white BMW 350i. It was a few years old, but it was paid for, and it was all hers. He'd also upgraded her living arrangements. After living in the hotel suite for a little over a month, Asia found a beautifully renovated townhouse in a small suburb outside of Philadelphia called Bala Cynwyd. It cost Waleek over three grand a month, but ... whatever Asia wanted, Asia got.

For the most part, they were happy, and Asia was thankful. They had their ups and downs, but nothing Asia couldn't handle. Their biggest issue was his late-night hours, and his stupid-ass baby-mama. Muff was the baby-mother from the fiery pits of hell. Every chance she got; she came with the bullshit. Though they hadn't run into each other since that first time in Germantown, Muff constantly sent threats through Waleek. Although he wouldn't relay them, Asia had heard her plenty of times yelling through the phone; calling her all kinds of bitches and ranting about how she would beat her ass. When she realized that those antics were unsuccessful, she somehow got ahold of Asia's number and began antagonizing her through phone calls, voicemail, and text messages.

Asia did her best not to entertain it; however, she was getting tired of the bullshit. Muff didn't want their daughter at the house and was making it hard for Waleek to see her. Things had to be on Muff's turf and time. Asia would hesitate to speak on it; however lately, it seemed that every time Waleek went to see his daughter, he stayed out later and later.

Asia shifted her thoughts back to Mitch as she drove her car down the highway to see him. She wasn't about to stress herself, worrying about what Waleek was doing. She was doing things differently this time. Mitch knew she had a new boyfriend and had told her that she needed to stop relying on niggas. A part of her wanted to believe that his ass was just jealous because she had moved on; however, Mitch made it clear that wasn't the case. He prided himself on being a man of morals and principles. He didn't expect Asia to put her life on hold for him. He was the one that had fucked up; not her. With that being said, Mitch encouraged her to live her life, but this time he wanted her to focus on stacking her paper and building a foundation that would support her even if she had no nigga.

Asia respected Mitch's opinion and was doing exactly what he said. She saved most of the money Waleek gave her and had gotten a part time job at a daycare downtown. She was even considering opening her own daycare. Mitch was glad that Asia was paying attention and heeding his advice. He wanted to make sure that she and their son were good. He hated that he hadn't left her in a better position financially. He told himself that if he ever got the opportunity, he would make sure they were set for life; no matter what he had to do.

A few hours later, Asia went through a security booth and was now headed down a long road around the prison perimeters. She had only been to the prison a few times since Mitch had arrived, and every time she seemed to hate it more. She parked her car, checked her attire, and went through everything that was in her purse. She didn't want to take anything in, or wear anything in, that could possibly stop her from seeing Mitch. Although they had been a couple for years, they were more than lovers and parents to Hasan; they were friends. She was genuinely excited to get a look at him and see how he was really doing.

"You ready baby?" she asked, while glancing back and looking at Hasan. He moved his lips in response and smiled. Surprisingly, he had managed to stay awake through the entire three-hour drive. She guessed he was just as excited as she was. She opened her door, hopped out of the front seat, and proceeded to unstrap him. "Let's go," she said.

ASIA SAT QUIETLY in the bright visiting room as she waited for Mitch to come out of the lone door that lead to the cellblocks and tiers of the prison. She held Hasan on her lap while she looked to the door anxiously. She glanced around the room periodically in nervousness, taking in the scene for what seemed like one too many times. Each time, she was never impressed. The state sure didn't give the inmates much to look forward to.

The room was large and open, with worn faded blue chairs lined up in long rows. Luckily, the visiting room wasn't packed, or they would have easily found themselves side-by-side and back-to-back with other inmates and their families. All the way at the bottom of the room was a kid section for inmates who had small children coming to visit. There were a few toys for them to play with, as well as a couple boxes of puzzles strewn on a brown, wooden table in the center of the aisle. For small children, it was common for them to become agitated and frustrated by the lengthy, oftentimes boring visits. At the top of the room, were a couple of large, old-fashioned, vending machines lined together. Some of them held sodas and juices, while the others had a selection of microwavable meals for the inmates to enjoy. Asia wouldn't dare say it was for the families to enjoy. The food looked disgusting; however, she had no doubt that the food the inmates regularly received, paled in comparison to it. For that reason, she spent nearly thirty dollars to make sure Mitch had more than a variety to choose from when he arrived. Individual carboard trays of chicken wings, mozzarella sticks, pizza, and anything else that looked edible were sitting beside her waiting for Mitch to come and get. She had even gathered up some napkins, paper plates, and condiments they had available. She wanted to give Mitch a little something to look forward to when he came out.

"Look at youuuuu!" she heard Mitch's strong, masculine voice say unexpectedly.

She had peered off for a few seconds and hadn't even seen him enter the room. Her eyes immediately lit up at the sight of him. He was still so fucking handsome, even in a dinghy-ass, burgundy state-issued, jump suit. Mitch had golden-brown skin, stood around six-foot, had a solid build with broad shoulders. Daily workouts had his body in impeccable shape. Waleek was fine. A whole snack ... but Mitch ... he was a fucking meal! A 220-pound meal

"Hey, Mitch!" she said, standing up with her son to hand him over.

"Wassup man!" Mitch said softly to Hasan after quickly scooping him from Asia's arms. Hasan was now smiling while being held in the air like a prized trophy. Mitch turned him from side to side to get a good look at him. He looked like he was being well cared for.

"He got big as shit," he said to Asia while he hugged her warmly. He was happy as hell to see them. He smiled at Asia. His eyes went from her face, then up and down her curvaceous body. She had gained some weight, but it had landed in all the right places. She always had a nice body, but now ... she had hips for days, fuller titties, and a fuller face. He couldn't wait until she turned around. He wanted to see how fat and wide that ass had gotten.

"You look good," he said, while taking his seat with his son in his lap.

"Thank you," she responded sheepishly. "You too." She noticed that he had a fresh, Caesar cut, and his beard was fuller. *Damn, you fine*, she thought, while she stared at him. As much as she hated to admit it, jail had been good for his body. She wished she could see it. Asia couldn't help but think about everything he used to do to her. Mitch adjusted in his seat and turned his attention to Asia, his gaze never wavering. His attention now made her nervous. It was weird how prison sentences had her feeling like he was damn near becoming a stranger. He had been gone a little over a year, but each visit became more awkward. Especially since he had been sentenced and they were no longer together.

"So, how you been?" he asked, noticing her growing uncomfortable. He had to catch himself from staring at her. Asia had been his first love. His only love. And he couldn't help how he still felt about her. Seeing her brought back so many memories. She looked so good and he just couldn't help but stare at the rare sight of beauty he was now deprived of daily.

Every day Mitch regretted that he had put himself in a position to be sitting in jail without Asia and his son. He had to keep himself from thinking about her being out in the world, getting fucked and turned out by some bitch-ass nigga. He had no doubt about it. Asia was a sexy ass broad. He remembered how often he would knock her back out as much as he could when he was home. She just had that quiet sex appeal.

"How you been holding up in here?" Asia asked.

While she did her best to make conversation, she was truly concerned about how Mitch was coping with the amount of time he was given. She loved Mitch, and although she knew he wasn't coming home anytime soon, she vowed that she would stick beside him, make his stay as comfortable as possible, and do everything she could to push for an appeal.

"I'm as good as I'm gon' get," he said, staring into her bright, round eyes. Asia looked at her son sitting in Mitch's arms and felt a stitch of sadness.

"Oh! I got you something to eat," she said, before leaning to her side and grabbing a plate. She took one of the forks and begin scooping food out of the containers and onto a plate for Mitch to enjoy.

"Thanks!" he said with a smile. He was thankful she had been thoughtful enough to grab it. He knew firsthand that the food in the visiting rooms was overpriced; however, he along with the other inmates enjoyed the occasional luxury.

While Mitch ate, Asia held their son while they talked and caught up. Although Mitch called home weekly and they spoke on the phone, they still had to play catch up on what was going on in the street, as well as Asia's life. Asia enjoyed her conversations with Mitch; that is, until he brought up something she didn't want to discuss: her love life.

"So, how things going with you and the nigga ... What did you say his name was again? Waleek?" he asked, knowing full well what his name was. Asia had told him multiple times.

Asia shifted around uncomfortably in her chair. She couldn't help but roll her eyes while sighing quietly. She didn't want to discuss another man with Mitch, especially because she still loved him. She always would. She didn't want to answer the question he'd just asked her because, despite how simple it sounded, it wasn't. However, she knew it was only fair, especially since she had their son Hasan around him. Mitch deserved to know what kind of relationship her and Waleek had. Asia glanced down a few feet away, where Hasan was close-by taking baby steps and playing with loose puzzle pieces.

"Things are going fine. He treats me well. He's good to Hasan," she finally responded. She paused and hoped that he didn't continue asking questions.

"That's wassup," he said, staring in her eyes and searching for any signs of dishonesty. He'd never had any problems with Asia lying to him; however, people changed daily. He also knew that although Asia wouldn't lie, she would withhold information. For that reason, he would just flat-out ask her whatever he wanted to know.

"So, he got y'all living out in Bala Cynwyd now, right? Remember what I told you about making sure you level up and establish a business or something in your name. That way, if shit goes sour... or he gets knocked, you got something solid to take care of yourself with."

"Yeah, I know. I'm working on it, Mitch," Asia said. While she appreciated his words of advice, she couldn't help but become slightly annoyed. The move she was trying to make, took time. She knew he genuinely wanted her to win, but she didn't want to be badgered about it.

"I've been looking at the qualifications and licenses required to open a daycare in the city. I've been talking to a few of the girls I work with."

"And?" Mitch asked, waiting for her to elaborate further on what she had come up with.

"Well, first, in order to open a daycare center that isn't in a home, I need a bachelor's degree. Which of course, I don't have."

"Okay. Well find someone that does, and partner up with them," he said, making it sound easier than what it was. "Just make sure that you have that paperwork ironed out by a lawyer. You want it to read that it's yo' shit at the end of the day."

"Yeah, I'm working on it. I can't go into business with just anybody; I gotta be able to trust them."

"Yeah, true," he said. He downed the last drop of soda he had left in the plastic bottle and put it to the side.

"Hayward!" the guard called out from the desk at the top of the room. It was where one officer sat and kept track of time, while the other patrolled the visiting room to make sure no fucking or drug smuggling was taking place.

"Times up!" the guard stated firmly, once he saw that he had gotten Mitch's attention. Mitch gave him a head nod to acknowledge the fact that he understood.

Asia sighed quietly in disappointment. She hated when the visits were up. She wished she could be there longer with him. It broke her heart every time they were forced to leave without him. He'd go back through that lone door. Back to count-times, lock-ins, and id numbers. She felt so helpless. She vowed that one day, she'd have enough money to get him an appeal. Despite its unlikelihood, they remained hopeful.

"Thanks for coming," Mitch said to Asia, as he stood up. He hugged her tightly, gave her a kiss on her temple, and then proceeded to hug his now sleeping son tightly.

After saying their good-byes, they watched Mitch disappear. Asia vowed to return soon. Since she now had a car, her intentions were to bring her son up there as often as she could. Visiting Mitch was never a problem. As long as Waleek never found out.

7

———————

M uff sucked and licked on the tip of Waleek's long, hard dick like it was her last meal. While she did that, she also focused on arching her ass above his face doggy-style. Despite having his pole stuffed in her mouth, she moaned while he went to work lapping at her pussy like the dog he was. As she reached her peak, she gyrated her ass down into his face; her juices dripping down onto his face. Muff wanted him to get every drop of goodness that was trickling from out of her pussy.

"Fuckkkkkk," she growled in sweet satisfaction, his dick inadvertently falling from her mouth. Waleek was a beast when it came to the head, and she made sure she got as much of it as she could every chance she got. She didn't give a damn what bitch he called himself being with.

"Suck that shit," he said once he felt Muff's lips come loose from his pole. He was just about to bust one and he needed her to keep going.

Muff used her tongue to lift his meat back up into her mouth. She went back to work bobbing up and down on his dick until he reached his climax.

"Damn!" he yelled out. As Muff continued to suck furiously, a euphoric feeling washed over him. He reached up and palmed her ass, pushing it down more into his face. He loved that freak shit and that's exactly why he fucked with Muff. He continued digging and swiping his tongue in, out and around her canal. He used one hand to smack her ass and the other to grip the side of her tiny waist. Waleek had come extra hard and now felt his member begin to deflate and soften up; however, like a Pitbull that had locked its jaws, Muff refused to let go. She kept sucking, making sure to swallow every drop of protein he had released, and had left behind.

"Mmmmmm," she said, licking her lips like she'd just had a feast.

Muff climbed off Waleek and walked into the hall to retrieve him a washcloth from the linen closet. Before she headed back into the room, she wet the washcloth in the bathroom and then passed it to him so he could clean himself up.

"Thanks," he said, taking the thick, cotton washcloth and running it up and down his private area. He wanted to rid himself of Muff's juices just in case Asia was on her bullshit. Every time he turned around; she was accusing him of fucking around; claiming that he reeked of pussy when he walked into the house.

Although he was guilty as charged, Waleek never gave her reasons to be suspicious. He wasn't a messy nigga; his problem was that he just happened to have a messy-ass baby-mother. Waleek began slipping back on his clothes while Muff walked back off into the bathroom to take a quick shower. Waleek went behind her to wash his face. He damn sure didn't want to return in the house with Muff all over his face and breath. He threw a couple of handfuls of water on his face and then used some paper towels nearby to dry it. He opened the cabinet underneath and pulled out the mouthwash. He knew exactly where everything was since Muff's house was practically his second home. After rinsing out his mouth, he went to his daughter Kayla's room and checked on her. She was still sprawled out, fast asleep on the twin-sized bed he'd just bought her a few weeks ago. Waleek went into the living room and plopped down on the couch to roll himself up a blunt. After about five minutes, Muff came out of the bathroom talking shit.

"You better tell that girlfriend of yours to stop fuckin' playing wit' me!" she demanded.

Waleek frowned his face up while he licked the sides of his blunt to seal it. "What the fuck is you talking about?" he asked.

"The bitch just text me talking shit!" she said, before jamming her iPhone in his face.

Waleek quickly read the message.

You thirsty bitches love to suck dick but don't got shit to show for it. While ya broke ass still in the projects, I'm in the suburbs hoe! Pretty bitches rest in the stixx. Bum bitches dream about!

Waleek shook his head. All it showed was Asia's message; however, he knew Muff had texted her first. That was the games Muff constantly played and that's exactly why him and Asia stayed going through bullshit. He should have been stopped fucking with Muff, but that mouth on her had a nigga in a chokehold. Muff was the modern-day super-head. She had lips that would wrap around a dick and choke the life out of them. And that tongue ... When that tongue slithered across his dick, it would damn near make a nigga's knees buckle. No matter how much he tried to stay away, the head kept him running back.

"Why the fuck do you keep texting her?" he asked, annoyed. "I know damn well she didn't text you first. You stay doing that shit. Now I'm gon' have to go home and hear this bullshit," he grumbled, before wrapping his lips around his blunt and pulling from it.

"Fuck you Waleek! You didn't tell me you went and got this bitch a house in the fucking county! But got me and ya fucking only child staying in fuckin' government housing!"

Waleek smacked his teeth while Muff stood in front of him butt-ass naked, demanding answers. "Come on Muff. Please don't start this shit," he groaned. "I give you more than enough money for you to have been got the fuck from round here. That's ya fault you fuck the bread up and choose to stay in the hood."

"I don't want to hear that shit Waleek! I want a new fuckin' crib by the end of the month or I'm telling that bitch every-thing!" she threatened. "I got video recordings of us fucking *and* you licking and sucking my ass nigga!"

Waleek turned and looked at Muff. He took a pull from his blunt and just stared at her. They had a love-hate relationship. And this was the part where the hate came in. This is the shit she did that he couldn't fucking stand. If she weren't his baby-mother, he would have been knocked her ass clean out.

"I'm not 'bout to play with you. Do some dumb shit and watch what happens," he told her. With his face in a scowl, he cut his eyes back at her.

"I don't want to hear that shit Waleek. Like I fuckin' said, I want a new crib by the end of the month!"

Muff walked off to put some clothes on, leaving Waleek sitting on the sofa in his thoughts. He took another pull from his blunt. He had only been with Asia three months and he was already dragging her through bullshit behind Muff. He knew she was growing tired of it. Despite giving her everything she wanted and needed, he knew it was only a matter of time before she rolled out on a nigga. He was going to move Muff into a new crib by the end of the month like she'd demanded. Not because he wanted her in a new crib; or because she deserved to be in a new crib. He was doing it because he didn't want her ghetto-ass fuckin' up his relationship with Asia. Asia was a better woman than Muff would ever be. She cooked, cleaned, kept a nice house, went to work, and school. On top of that, she was an excellent mother. He'd be stupid to fuck that up. He knew he needed to get shit together fast. He could only imagine what Muff had sent her to prompt Asia to even respond. He also knew that Asia's baby-father had been in her ear.

Waleek had heard through the grapevine that Mitch had been inquiring about him, and he didn't like it one fucking bit. He didn't have a squeaky-clean past and he also hadn't been completely upfront about it with Asia. He didn't want Mitch meddling in his private affairs and fucking shit up for him ... on any levels.

"I'm tired of that bitch!" Asia yelled, as she stormed around her spacious room slamming shit. "The bitch sent me a picture of your dick Waleek! A picture of your fucking dick!" she repeated for emphasis. "It went from her running her mouth and sending threats, to her sending me trifling ass, dick pictures! When is this shit gonna stop Waleek? I don't know how much more of the disrespect I can take!" she screamed.

Waleek sighed. He wished Asia would quiet down. They lived in a swanky, little townhouse community and he didn't want the neighbor's all up in their business. He was glad his mother had already left for work. She too also lived there with them. Nothing would have satisfied his mother more than to see Asia crying, fussing, and carrying on. She wasn't particularly fond of their relationship; especially because Asia didn't have much of anything accumulated on her own, *and* she had a baby in tow with her. His mother wasn't keen on him taking care of someone else's child.

"That was probably an old ass picture Asia! I haven't fucked with Muff since we been together!" he lied, as he sat hunched over the bed.

He used his left foot to push off his right Timberland. He had just walked in the house and Asia was going off. He knew it was coming though. That's exactly why he made a pit stop before he got to their spacious, luxury townhome, smackdab in the suburbs of Bala Cynwyd.

Waleek removed his shirt and tossed it on the California King sized bed. He headed out to take a shower but before he could walk out of the room, Asia had reared up in his face and was now blocking his path. With her face in an angry grimace, she leaned up and mushed his forehead with her index finger.

"That picture was recent! Save the bullshit!" she yelled. "Why the fuck are you wit' me if you gon' keep fucking with that bitch?" she asked.

Asia didn't understand the stupid ass games they played. Some of the shit Muff presented to her was so silly and childish that she didn't even know what, *or* who to believe. The same boxers he had on then were also the same boxers that were in the picture that Muff had sent. Waleek either didn't give a fuck, or he thought she was just plain ol' stupid.

"Babe, please," Waleek pleaded. He wrapped his arms gently around her waist and tried to reason with her. However, she immediately shoved them down from around her.

"Get the fuck off me! Don't fucking touch me! You were just laid up with that bitch! I saw the boxers Waleek!"

Waleek sighed and shook his head in frustration. He was tired and had a long day, if he weren't dealing with the drama on the streets, he was dealing with drama from his baby-mom or drama at home. He had to figure out a way to get Muff in line.

"Yo, don't let that bitch get to you ... She just mad because she doesn't have your spot. Instead of being with her, I'm with you. She gon' do any and everything to get under your skin. Don't let that bitch trick you out yo' spot!"

Asia smacked her teeth before walking off and sitting on the bed. She buried her head in her hands. At this point, the way Asia was feeling; Muff could have Waleek's ass back. Yeah, he had good dick and some fire-ass head, but she hadn't signed up to get cheated on, antagonized, and damn near taunted every day by his stupid ass baby-mama. They'd only been together three months, and while Waleek treated her like a princess when they were together, she was constantly reminded that he was nothing more than a dog ass nigga when she wasn't present. She didn't want a nigga like that. She wanted a nigga that was loyal. She knew that Waleek was a hustler when she met him; she expected him to fuck bitches, but she also expected him to keep them the fuck in line. Muff was a problem.

Although, Waleek gave her damn near everything she needed and wanted, she wanted nothing more than to be left the fuck alone. She wanted respect! She never had to deal with shit like this from Mitch. Mitch would air her out if he even knew she was tolerating this shit from another nigga.

"Waleek, I am tired of this shit," she said, fighting extra hard to keep tears from leaking from her eyes. She wasn't about to keep letting nobody's punk-ass son keep fucking with her emotions like that.

"I swear, I will pack my shit up and leave," she threatened.

Even though she said it, she hardly even believed herself. Where would she go? What would she do? She had some money saved, but it wasn't enough to maintain a household for long. Sure, she had a job, but working at the daycare center didn't pay much more than minimum wage. *I can always sell my car*, she thought. However, that thought quickly dissipated when she realized how much easier life became after getting it.

Despite her fight, tears managed to force their way from her eyes and down her cheeks. She wiped them away angrily and sniffled silently. Waleek didn't say anything. He walked in front of Asia and knelt in front of her so he could be eye-level with her.

"Asia, look at me," he said. "There's nobody I want more than you. All that shit she says is lies. Muff has been an issue with every chick I've ever dealt with. She's lied to *every* chick I ever fucked with. Stop feeding into that shit babe," he said softly. "Look up at me," he pleaded.

He took his hand and lifted her head up. Her beautiful face was tear streaked. He hated to see her cry, and he hated even more that he was the sole cause of it. He cared about Asia a lot, but there wasn't a chick on earth that was going to make him be 100 percent faithful. It just wasn't in his nature or man's nature period. He was going to make sure that Muff became less of an issue; and he was going to do that soon. Waleek wanted Asia to be happy, but he also still wanted to do whatever he wanted.

"Stop letting her get to you. It's all lies," he reassured her.

With tears still rolling down her face, she nodded in agreement. A part of her wanted to believe him; yet a part of her didn't. She had always been told never to take a bitch's word over her nigga's. As much as her gut told her not to, she was going to rock with her nigga on this one. If she didn't catch them fucking with her own eyes, she wasn't going to believe it.

"Okay," she said. She lifted her hand and wiped away the tears on her face.

"Gimme kiss," Waleek said, leaning his head in towards Asia. She complied. Pulling away with a smile, Waleek got up and went into his back pocket. He pulled out a blue Tiffany and Co. box and handed it to her.

"I got you something," he said.

Asia took the box and inspected it. "What's in it?" she asked.

"Open it," he encouraged.

He knew she would like what she saw. She had seen the bracelet about a week ago. He could have bought it then, but he figured he would grab it later. As soon as he left Muff's house earlier that day, he knew then it would be the perfect time. He wasted no time sliding by the Tiffany and Co. downtown to do a little damage control.

Asia opened the box and instantly lit up. It was the gold Tiffany T bracelet that she wanted; only this one had diamonds in it. The one she wanted was $1,900. She knew this one had to cost every bit of three grand.

"It's beautiful," she gushed. "Thank you, babe," she said.

She put it on her arm and admired the shiny metal against her caramel skin. It was gorgeous. As much as she wanted to stay mad, she couldn't. She wasn't even certain that he had cheated; however, she did know that if he was really cheating, then accepting his gift was merely encouraging his infidelity. It was stating that she could be bought.

Asia decided that she was going to change her number in the morning. She was tired of Muff. She was going to get on top of her game. If Waleek *was* cheating, she wanted to be able to walk away like a real bitch could.

"How he still getting money if he told on niggas?" Mitch asked his cell-buddy Shareef.

"Mannnnn ... I don't even fuckin' know. Nigga's ain't solid like how they used to be," he said shaking his head. "They claim they don't fuck with rats, but if the money right, they fuck wit 'em anyway." Shareef, a skinny, light skinned cat from North Philly, sat on the edge of the bottom bunk he occupied and continued his crossword puzzle.

"And you say you don't remember the name of the boy he told on?" Mitch asked again.

"Na. I just heard he told on some white boy from South Philly. I don't really know too much about him. I just heard his name before and that he was fuckin' with them white mufuckas out South Philly. They don't even usually fuck with nigga's, but they fucked with him, and somehow, someway he got busted and then, so did they. He did a lil' bit but whoever he told on, they got football numbers."

"Damn." Mitch rested his back against the hard, concrete wall quietly. He wasn't going to continue prying. He appreciated the information that he'd gotten thus far; however, it didn't seem like he knew much more than what he'd already given.

Mitch had inquired about Waleek the very first time Asia had brought his name up. He wanted to be briefed on the nigga that was now shacking up with his bitch and his son. The things he was hearing about Waleek however, weren't at all good. Word on the street was he was a snitch. Mitch couldn't understand how he was still getting money. That was another thing he'd heard as well; that Waleek definitely secured the bag. Mitch couldn't help but feel a wave of jealousy creep through his veins. He knew the hoe ass nigga was dicking down his girl daily. As bad as Asia was, he knew the nigga was beating that ass down every chance he got. Mitch knew first-hand how tempting Asia was. He didn't want no nigga taking care of his family, but what choice did he have? He was locked up, and the way things were going, he wasn't going to be getting out anytime soon.

Mitch wanted to tell Asia about what he heard; however, he decided to wait. He wanted to get some more information on him first. With his loose-fitting jumpsuit, he moved away from the wall and laid his body flat down on his bunk. The thin twin-size mattress provided nothing more than a weak barrier against the metal it laid atop. Mitch could still feel it. He did his best to make himself comfortable. Forcing his eyes shut, he decided he would try to get some sleep. Instead of worrying about what Asia and his son were doing without him; he figured he would allow the memories they had before he left fill his thoughts instead.

8

———

Asia walked around the Gucci store in the King of Prussia Mall and quietly scanned the aisles. There was so much shit to choose from, she didn't know where to begin. She picked up a white, silk blouse with a bow in the front and held it up in front of her to inspect the design. As she looked it over, she noticed that the price attached to it said $900. *Damn, for a plain ass white blouse*, she thought to herself. Luckily, Waleek had given her $10,000 to shop with. If she knew the stores were this expensive, she would have asked for $20,000. Since being with Waleek, Asia's lifestyle had changed. Instead of wearing Rainbow and Forever 21, she now wore Gucci, Prada, and Chanel. Waleek bought most of it while he was out shopping for himself. This was the first time she had went out and bought her own high-end apparel and she was sticker shocked.

After hawking over a few items, Asia settled on a wallet, a belt, and a pair of boots. Her total came to $2,100. She hadn't even come to the mall to do any shopping. She'd really come just to visit the Apple store. She wanted to upgrade her phone. Apple was directly across from the Gucci store at The King of

Prussia Mall, so after paying for her items, Asia grabbed her bags and headed over. The logo stamped white, paper shopping bags she carried rubbed together noisily as she made her exit. Just as she was leaving out, she damn near ran smack dab into the last person on Earth she ever wanted to see: Muff and two of her side kicks. She recognized one of them as Kareema, Muff's best friend. The other she'd never seen before.

Asia rolled her eyes and out of instinct, curled her lip up in distaste. Muff didn't miss the funky ass look Asia gave. As much as she wanted to honor Waleek's request to leave the bitch alone, she couldn't. She hated how Asia walked around like she was better than everyone.

"Frown ya face up again bitch," Muff mumbled loud enough so Asia could hear her.

"And what?" Asia responded, surprising Muff and her homegirls. Asia had barely gotten out the front of the Gucci store and Muff was already running her mouth. Her and the broke bitches with her, had her fucked up. She didn't have her son today and she had time. Contrary to Muff's belief, Asia was far from pussy. Muff sent threats all day over the phone, but if the bitch really wanted to pop off, then it could happen.

"What!" Muff replied, immediately growing angry. *This bitch act like I won't beat her high-siddity ass the fuck up,* she thought to herself.

"You made a remark about how my face looked when I looked at you and ya fuckin' flunkies," Asia replied boldly.

The remark shocked Muff and her friends. Her homegirls looked at Muff like she'd better not let some punk-ass, high-yellow-hoe talk to her all crazy.

"Bitch ain't neither one of us a mafuckin' flunky. The same way you shopping, we shopping," Kareema responded.

She too didn't like Asia. The bitch had been a problem for Muff since she came into the picture. It also didn't help that Waleek kept the hoe laced, seemingly shitting on her friend

Muff. Every time he came around, he had his face tore up as if he looked down on them. He acted like he had upgraded so much; when in reality, Asia was a hoodrat just like everybody else.

"Right. Don't get it twisted. The nigga you run around here and claim as yo' man, is the same nigga that got me in here shopping too," Muff threw in. "And he the same nigga that slobs down this pussy on the regular like it's his last fuckin' meal," she replied with a giggle.

Asia felt her blood run hot. Deep down she knew the statement was true. She had no wins in a verbal spar against Muff, so she decided she wasn't going to continue arguing back and forth with her. She had no desire to be embarrassed any more than what she already was.

"Whatever bitch," she grumbled and turned her back. Before she could even take a few steps to begin walking off, she felt a forceful fist against her head, followed by a fury of more fists.

Asia instantly dropped her bags and purse to the ground and went into fight mode. As she spun around throwing her hands, Muff instantly went for her long hair to pull her down to the ground. Asia had expected it and had already thrown back her head to escape Muff's lunge. Muff swung wildly and quickly like the wild, ghetto broad she was; however, she wasn't a heavy weight. She was petite; standing five-three and weighing no more than 150-pounds, compared to Asia's 170.

Asia managed to overpower her quickly, while Kareema and their other friend rained punches down on her and swung her across the slippery mall floor like a rag doll. Although Asia knew she didn't have much wins, she stayed leveled on her feet and swung her hands like a Philly bitch would. She refused to let them drag her to the ground, and she refused to stop fighting. With her head up and eyes open, Asia threw down mercilessly until she felt security lift the three women off her.

"It's on sight bitch!" Asia screamed after being violently attacked by the three dusty bitches.

Her five-hundred-dollar weave was all over her head, she had a cut above her eye, and she could taste a tinge of blood in her mouth. She was tired of Muff fucking with her. She was glad they had tried her; now they would know what the fuck it was and what she stood for. She wasn't a pussy-ass bitch and her pretty ass could stand amongst the toughest bitches. Next time she saw Muff, she was going to beat her ass.

"I don't give a fuck bitch!" Muff yelled out. She was always ready for smoke. If Asia wanted it, she could get it anytime. She had to admit; she didn't expect Asia to be able to brawl. For her to be able to stand her ground against all three of them, was impressive.

After being asked some questions and declining to answer them, Asia got ready to be escorted to her car. Although it was clear she could handle herself, it was routine procedure by mall security after an altercation. As Asia went to leave, she scooped up her purse and then she looked around for her two Gucci bags with the items she'd just bought. However, she only saw one. She then realized that Muff or one of her broke ass friends, had swiped her bag. She really didn't see Muff doing it. Muff wore high-end shit on the regular basis, just like she did. Asia shook her head angrily. How in the hell could that broke bitch, afford to shop in the Gucci store like she did? Something told her that Waleek was still fucking her. Something had to give, or she was ready to give up.

9

____

Waleek stood in his trap house and leaned his back against the faded, off-white, paint-chipped wall. He watched carefully as fiends entered and exited like clockwork. He had two sets of bando's, and both ran the same way. This one was on a dead-end block, around the corner from his other two on Pulaski street. Both were large, two story, abandoned duplexes that nobody had lived in for years. Combined, he had a total of four houses.

Waleek watched as a pair of white, junkie broads, took turns tying each other's arms up. He could see the excitement, eagerness, and anticipation displayed in their eyes. They were desperate to take a hit. They'd heard about the shit that was being sold out of the spot they were in. They'd heard it was so good, it felt like your soul left your body. They wanted to feel it. They wanted the experience. No one could turn down a high like that. For that exact reason, fiends were lined up, and were in and out of both his spots constantly. Waleek was doing numbers. He was easily making $20,000 a day from each spot. After paying his workers and buying more product, he took home at least $10,000 a night. He just hoped that it stayed that way.

A couple of his youngins had come to him and said that rumors were circulating in the street. Rumors of him being a rat and getting a nigga cased up in South Philly. Waleek was a firm believer in the old saying: *believe none of what you hear and only half of what you see.* The alleged, Ricardo had gotten himself cased up for being reckless and stupid. Waleek had just been caught up by association. He was never under any type of surveillance until he started fucking around with him. Yeah, he had caught a case years ago, but the charge in question was specifically related to Ricardo's bullshit.

Waleek had only been buying large amounts of dope off him for six months before the feds were raiding his mother's crib. Ricardo's name was the first one they dropped. They made it very clear that he was the one they wanted and not Waleek. They already knew who Ricardo was dealing with, where he got his shit from and where he slung it. He knew he was under surveillance before he took Waleek under his wing. Being the type of nigga that he was; he wasn't feeling that shit. Ricardo had been greedy and in order to make money, he had other people slinging his shit even though he was hot and messy. Waleek never approached Ricardo for a deal. Ricardo came to him. It all made sense when the Feds schooled him on why the white boys liked to fuck with the blacks. They were a lot more loyal. Loyal to a fault. The white boys would take the poorest nigga with potential out of the trenches, and put him on, like they'd done something for him. When shit hit the fan, that same broke nigga would often keep his mouth closed out of loyalty. *Fuck that,* Waleek thought. He was going to be loyal to himself; not some bitch-ass white boy who lead him right into the lion's den.

Waleek didn't give a fuck if nigga's screamed that he was a rat. At the end of the day, he was a real nigga and he'd lay anybody the fuck down. Waleek's problem was, he didn't want that rat shit getting in the way of his money. Fiends would still buy his shit because it was the best around; however, there were other issues that he wasn't sure if he would be able to avoid. For starters, most niggas that told were considered bitch-ass-niggas. That left him vulnerable to the stick-up kids and jack-boys who liked to take down trap spots. A couple of his young boys had already been strong-armed for their shit. That was already a sign of blatant disrespect. Waleek now had everyone strapped up and ready, just in case some shit like that happened again. He couldn't have a weak team. He couldn't let shit keep sliding. If any person on his team was considered weak; they would likely be seen weak as a complete whole. And he was far from weak.

Waleek continued to watch as his business continued to run systematically. He observed all the addicts come through the back. They didn't use a door at this location. Instead, they entered through a gaping hole in the side of the house. After being abandoned and neglected for so long, the bricks on one of the houses began to crumble. Waleek had one of the dope fiends chip the rest away, until a hole was formed. For things to run smoothly and systematically, as soon as they entered, they walked down a long hall and got in line. At the top of the line, he had his strongest and most vicious worker taking the money, while another would distribute the product once they paid for it. Also, in the back of that room, sat another two of his workers. They were heavily armed since they held on to the larger part of the shipment, as well as oversaw organizing and handing out bundles. One of their most important tasks was to guard the work. In the adjacent house, fiends were given thirty-minutes to either snort or shoot up their drugs. Once that thirty-minutes was up, they had to roll.

Waleek also designated the use of a few rooms, for those who needed a quick place to fuck so they could make some more money. It wasn't uncommon to walk into a room and see three or four couples engaged in some type of sexual activity. It all helped Waleek's business thrive. He wouldn't allow anything that didn't. The fiends loved it; since to them, the place was almost a one stop shop. They could buy drugs, find someplace safe to smoke, and then meet in one of the rooms too if they needed to earn some money to do the shit all over again. Waleek didn't discriminate. Normally it was women that fucked for money but lately, there had been a few instances where it was the other way around.

Waleek's places were a drug addicts paradise, and the concept was going to get him rich. All he needed was a couple more houses just like the one he was in, spread out through the city. Being based in Germantown was keeping him fed, but if he wanted to get fat, he needed to branch off and set up shop in North Philly. He just wasn't sure how he planned to do that yet. Especially since people were going around throwing dirt on his name. Waleek knew it was only a matter of time before nigga's started to throw his past up in his face.

Muff clenched her vaginal muscles together tightly and slid up and down Zee's pole. He wasn't incredibly large, but he had a curve and the angled dick was hitting, had Muff's eyes ready to hit the back of her head and stay there. She was a borderline nymphomaniac. She loved fucking and sucking dick. She loved it even more when she was compensated for it.

"Sh-ittttttt," she groaned, her body pulsating and tingling from her powerful climax. Her mouth hung open in awe, but no words came out. Zee responded by thrusting his hips upwards and gripping the bottom of Muff's waist, so she could continue gliding up and down his member forcefully. He ignored the droplets of sweat trickling down the front of his face.

"Damn," he grumbled in pleasure. For Muff, the phrase came like clockwork. Anybody she fucked, always said the same shit. She had some good pussy and some remarkable head.

Zee let out a few breathy grunts and a few seconds later, reached a climax. "Fuckkkkkk," he growled, his lean body stiffening up. For a few seconds he sat there frozen in place. *This bitch is a beast*, he thought to himself. Feeling his dick begin to deflate, he proceeded to pat Muff's thigh, so she could get up.

Muff climbed off and collapsed beside him. She threw her leg across his long, lean torso and began stroking his chest. Although she had only been seeing him for a few weeks, she liked Zee. Slender with cream-colored skin, he wore his hair low and curly. He was fifty percent Puerto Rican and fifty percent African American. Being from South Philly, he wasn't familiar with Muff's reputation; luckily for her. If he had heard about her, he probably would have steered clear. He had heard of Waleek's reputation though.

"I gotta get ready to meet my baby-father in a few," she said, noticing that Zee was getting too comfortable. His eyes were closed, and he was sprawled out with his hands behind his head. If she left him alone, she had no doubt that he'd be sleep in a couple of minutes. She had a way of putting nigga's out.

"Well, go meet him," he said. He didn't care about whatever it was she was talking about; he just needed ten-minutes to catch some shut-eye.

"He's coming here," she said.

After he failed to respond, she nudged him again and got out the bed to take a quick shower and meet Waleek. She had just found a new house and was moving in within a day or two. He had already given her over $6,000 for the first month, last month, and security deposit. She was hoping to get another five from him tonight so she could go furniture shopping. Although Waleek had suspicions, he didn't know anything about Zee, and she wanted to keep it that way.

Even though Waleek had a girlfriend, He too had jealous ways. He didn't want Muff fucking anyone, and he especially didn't want them anywhere near his daughter.

"Come on Zee baby, get up," she pled. God forbid Waleek come in and see him there.

Zee cracked open his eyes slightly and finally responded. He was tired. He'd been making moves all day and then Muff begged him to come over. After sucking the life out of him, she was basically putting a nigga out. He forced himself up out the bed and yawned loudly. He scanned the floor and spotted his clothes in a corner. He had stripped down to nothing. Sliding his legs in his jeans he began to get dressed.

"I got my nigga's outside waiting on me anyway," he said aloud to no one in particular. He almost forgot he'd brought along his seventeen-year-old, little cousin, and his sidekick.

After getting dressed, he called out to Muff to let her know he was leaving. "Come put this deadbolt on the door!" he shouted, not realizing Muff's daughter Kayla, was sleeping in the back. He opened the door and stood there, waiting for a response. He was about to walk off, but then he heard the bathroom door open, followed by Muff's voice.

Now finished with her shower, Muff exited the bathroom with a towel tied tightly around her. Her skin was still damp, and her long weave cascaded loosely down her back. Zee stared at her and smiled. As ghetto as she sometimes acted, she was picture perfect.

"I know you wasn't going leave without giving me a kiss," she said, walking towards him with a seductive grin.

She stood on her tip toes, while Zee leaned down and pressed his lips into hers. He palmed her ass tightly before pulling his lips away from hers and smiling. *Ya lil' ass like crack,* he thought to himself. Something about Muff was addictive. Muff smiled sweetly but her face instantly changed when she heard her daughter's cry and then her subsequent footsteps. She smacked her teeth when she saw Kayla stumbling in the living room, half-sleep, and half-whining. She wiped her eyes in frustration while she peered around for her mother. Kayla had heard her voice and followed it. Initially, it was the sound of Zee's voice yelling through the house that woke her up.

"Mommyyyyy!" she cried.

Muff smacked her teeth silently. She had given Kayla some Nyquil not long ago, so she wasn't sure why her ass was even up so soon. The medicine should have had her down for hours. Still crying as she approached, Muff scooped Kayla up into her arms and patted her back gently.

Zee smiled. "I see you busy. I'ma let you go," he said. He leaned down and gave her another kiss while she held her daughter. Out of habit, when Muff kissed, she closed her eyes. However, when she opened them, she wished she had kept them shut. Waleek was walking towards her front door and his facial expression displayed nothing short of fury.

10

———

"**B**itch! What the fuck is you doing?" Waleek growled, his eyes glaring brightly with anger. When he walked up and saw Muff standing at the door with some Puerto Rican-looking nigga it took everything out of him not to break his foot off in her ass.

"What da fuck is you doing with nigga's in front of yo' crib with my daughter in yo' fucking arms!" Waleek yelled to Muff as he approached. He knew he should have kept his cool, but he immediately lost it. Waleek didn't even bother acknowledging Zee since he didn't really have any issues with him. His issue was with the mother of his child.

"I gotta go," Muff said quietly, walking away from the door.

Zee wasn't impressed with Waleek and all the theatrics, but he didn't say a word. He didn't like to participate in domestic disputes, since they could turn ugly very quickly.

"Who da fuck is this nigga?" Waleek yelled as he stepped into the house. Here he was, bringing Muff money so she could buy furniture for the house he just got her, and she just finished sucking dick. *Bitch should have sucked that nigga dick for some money instead of spending my shit*, he thought angrily.

"I'm out Mami!" Zee yelled. "Hit me up when things calm down," he said. "*Rat ass nigga's always do the most*," he mumbled.

Waleek had no intention of saying anything to Zee until he opened his mouth and made the comment. Zee didn't even realize his thoughts had come out verbally. He also didn't realize he said it loud enough for Waleek to hear him. However, the comment was heard, and it didn't go unnoticed *or* unaddressed.

"What the fuck you say pussy!" Waleek screamed out.

"Zee just go, please!" Muff screamed. Shit was about to get physical and for the first time, she didn't have time for the drama. She ushered her daughter to her room, so she wouldn't have to hear the drama she caused.

"Nah! Let that pussy repeat the shit he just said!" Waleek challenged.

"Whatever nigga," Zee laughed. He didn't have any respect for nigga's that told. Instead of walking off like he had intended, he stood there and mugged Waleek. Hearing bits of the commotion, his little cousin and friend hopped out of the parked black, Dodge Magnum they were in and begin walking up.

"Yeah, that's what the fuck I thought," he said. Waleek had heard the whispers but out of respect and fear, no one had mentioned it; let alone dare repeat it or say it to his face. Through the open door, Waleek saw the niggas walking up. He immediately knew that shit was about to go left. All he'd come to do was see his daughter and bring Muff some money. He'd let his temper get the best of him and now he was only left with two choices. He could stay in the house and wait for the three niggas to leave, or he could leave now. He chose the latter.

"Fuck you bitch," Waleek spat. "I'm leaving and not giving you shit. Get it from the broke ass nigga you fuckin'," he said. He pushed past Zee and walked through the door.

"Fuck you Waleek!" Muff spat. She couldn't stand his jealous tantrums. He had a whole fucking girlfriend and got to fuck whoever he wanted, but as soon as she started fucking with someone, it was a problem. He was quick to say he wasn't going to do anything for her, or he wasn't giving her any money. She was tired of it.

"Better watch where the fuck you going," Zee's little cousin demanded, while standing by his side. He stared Waleek down coldly, as he walked off and back towards his car.

"Fuck you, nigga!" Waleek spat, while continuing to walk off. Before he could take another three steps, he felt the butt of a gun come down violently on his head. That gun belonged to Zee.

Waleek spun around in pain and found himself face-to-face with all three of the men. He went to run but was hit again; this time on the side of his face. Instead of fighting back, Waleek struggled to break free. He knew he didn't have any wins against all three men. He knew there was at least one gun amongst the men. He wasn't sure if all of them were holding. Out of instinct, he reached for his revolver. He never left home without it. He felt a barrage of fists coming down on him as he continued to snatch his gun from out his waist band. A second later he managed to pull it free. He snatched his hand back furiously, lifted his gun in the air, and pulled the trigger.

Pow! Pow! Pow!

Waleek fired his gun to get the three men off him. Although Zee had a gun, he didn't expect Waleek to have one. By the time the men realized he was armed, they were already at a disadvantage. Waleek had put distance between them and they were in the middle of the street clear as day. Waleek now had a clear shot. All they could do was run. Zee's cousin and friend took off and ran back towards the car. They tumbled to the ground for safety and kneeled on the side to get out of the way of Waleek's firearm.

Zee ran back towards Muff's apartment to try and put some distance between him and Waleek so he could fire back. The problem was; he should have never turned his back on Waleek. Just as he was approaching the front of Asia's apartment, Waleek leveled his gun down and fired on him. The bullet pierced the back of Zee's head and dropped him down right in front of the door. Seeing Zee's body fall, Waleek took off running.

"Ahhhhhhhhhhhh!" Muff's hi-pitched screams could be heard through the neighborhood. During the commotion, she never closed her door. She threw her hand over her mouth in horror when she saw Zee fall directly in front of her apartment. He now lay lifeless with a pool of bright, red blood collecting around his head.

Hearing the commotion, neighbors began to peek out their window, while others began to dial 911. Hearing the shots go off and then the screams, they knew it had to be bad. In the city of Philadelphia, it meant that somebody was injured or worse: dead.

Shit. Shit. Shit, Waleek thought to himself as he hopped in his car and barreled down the block frantically. He knew he was fucked. He just killed someone and left two witnesses. Although something told him to go straight home to Bala Cynwyd, he instead fled to his Aunt Joyce's house. That would be his worse mistake. His aunt lived in the hood and that also happened to be what he had listed as his primary address in the police database. That was the first place the police went to pick him up. He had been identified after the police responded to a homicide. They locked Waleek up in front of his aunt and his mother after she had pulled up after being called by her sister. Waleek was charged with first degree murder. He was royally fucked.

11

It was nearly seven-thirty in the evening when Asia walked in the door of her home and kicked off her shoes by the entryway. The rush hour traffic had been especially brutal. Since it was Friday, it seemed like the drivers were unusually aggressive and eager to end their week. Apparently, so eager that causing a collision was the least of their worries. Tailgating and excessive speeding were just a few of the things she had to deal with.

Asia left her work bag by the door, walked into the living room and sunk down into the cushions of the plush, oversized couch. Thankfully, she had dropped Hasan off to Mitch's mother and was kid free for the weekend. Yet, she still had no desire to do anything else other than relax. Leaning her body against the back of the couch, she smiled. She had the house all to herself and she was going to enjoy it. Waleek was out trappin' and by the grace of God, his mother Carolyn was gone to work. She worked the second shift at the hospital, and although she lived there with them, they didn't see much of her. When she was there, she was as quiet as a church mouse, and when she was off, she was always with her sister somewhere. Asia was glad. She preferred it that way. She wasn't a big fan of Carolyn and she flat out disliked her sister Joyce. While Carolyn at least tolerated Asia on the strength of Waleek, Joyce made it clear that she didn't like Asia. She had expressed on multiple occasions to Waleek that she felt that Asia was nothing more than a gold-digging hoe.

Asia sat up and was about to go in her room and get some of that good-ass, loud Waleek kept in the back, but her ringing phone kept her from doing anything.

"Damn," I just got in the house, she grumbled, before hopping to her feet to retrieve her phone from her purse that she'd left on the accent table that sat next to the front door.

She quickly rummaged through her bag and found her phone. It was vibrating and ringing like crazy. She looked down at the flashing screen and didn't recognize the number. She rolled her pretty eyes and prepared to bang on a bill collector. However, the message that came through the phone when she answered, seemed to cause time to stand still.

"You have a collect call from Waleek Brown, at the Philadelphia ..."

Asia felt a wave of nausea pass over her. That quickly things became a blur. She blinked a few times to make sure she wasn't sleep and once she realized she wasn't, she waited for the automated system to stop talking. She quickly pressed the number after being prompted and waited for the sound of Waleek's voice to come through.

"Asia!" Waleek said loudly through all the background noise. He was happy she had picked up. He needed her on top of shit as soon as possible.

"Waleek! What the fuck happened?" Asia asked, her heart hammering in her chest. Her thoughts began running wildly. She wondered what he'd gotten caught with. She was sure he had been caught with drugs. Was he driving? Was he on the block? Did somebody snitch? Was it one of his homies that snitched?! She needed answers, and she needed them now!

"Listen Asia, and listen carefully," Waleek said firmly. He glanced over his shoulder to make sure no one was listening. Nowadays, if nigga's thought you had money and could come up, they'd get your people hit from inside. All nigga's thought about was finding ways to come up. It didn't matter how they did it or who they crossed.

"Look, you gotta set up an account with Global Tel. Use ya bank card to do it; and do it soon. This call gonna hang up soon. It's just a courtesy."

"What are you in there for?" Asia asked, gripping the phone tightly against her ear. It felt as if all the breath in her body was being sucked right from the center of her chest. She couldn't believe Waleek was in jail.

"It's not for drugs. They tryin' to put a body on me," he admitted.

"A body!" Asia screamed.

"Asia calm down. Listen to me! I need you to keep it together; hold things down for a bit. I didn't do shit and I'm gonna fight this shit. Grab the bag, switch the spot, and move the money. You gonna drop twenty on my lawyer Monday. They probably not gon give me a bail but I'm gon' still push for it," he said solemnly.

"Fuck Waleek," Asia muttered. Shit was a lot realer than she thought.

"You have thirty seconds," the automated voice chimed in and let them know that their call was just about up.

"Asia, handle that shit asap. I love you and I'll call tomorrow. Don't worry about calling my folks. I already talked to my mom and she know you got shit under control. Just get the money and get on top of my lawyer asap!" he exclaimed. He couldn't stress enough how important his lawyer was.

Asia and Waleek quickly said their good-byes before the

phone clicked. As soon as the phone hung up, Asia screamed out in frustration. "Fuck!" she yelled.

She grabbed her wallet containing her debit card from her purse. She figured she would go ahead and set up the prepaid calling account. Staying on top of things made life easier. He had literally just rambled off a list of things for her to do and she didn't want to forget anything. Still clutching her phone, she walked over to the couch and setup the account. When she was done, she looked at her phone to see what time it was. Although it was now only a little after eight, Asia had no desire to do anything else other than go to sleep. She went into her spacious master bath and retrieved a sleep aid from her medicine cabinet. She figured it would put her down for eight hours so she would be back up and ready to handle shit by five a.m.

THE NEXT MORNING Asia was up by four-thirty a.m. She took a shower, threw on her clothes, and got on the road. The first place she went, was to a storage facility out in West Chester, PA; an affluent suburban community west of Philadelphia. To be safe, Waleek didn't keep money in the house; he instead kept it in a storage facility in a lily-white suburb, where crime was almost non-existent. Asia pulled into the storage facility and drove around to the small unit that Waleek had gotten her to rent for him. Previously, his mother Carolyn, had always gotten the storage units for him. Not long after they begin dating, Asia had convinced him to let her handle storing his cash. The most important lesson she learned when Mitch fell, was that if the girlfriend had no access to a nigga's money, she was just as good as fucked if he got knocked. She vowed to never let that happen again. She had been handling Waleek's money for about two months now. He trusted her so much, he wasn't even sure of the exact count. He left that up to her.

Asia slid the metal door up and rummaged through the boxes that Waleek had lying around. The unit contained mostly shoe boxes and plastic totes that held Waleek's summer clothes. Asia continued scanning the unit until she found the tote she was looking for. She didn't bother to open it. She simply dragged it out of storage and lifted it into her trunk. She looked at the rest of the boxes and totes still inside. She had no choice but to move it all. It didn't make sense to rent two storages. Besides, it would look not only ridiculous, but also suspicious if she rented a whole unit just for one lone tote. Asia went back in the storage unit and proceeded to clear out everything inside. Luckily, it wasn't too much. Everything was able to fit in her car with ease. After locking up, she drove off and pulled around to the front office, so she could let them know that she no longer needed the unit. After terminating her rental agreement, she headed over to a similar storage facility on the other side of town and purchased a new rental. She paid it up for several months and then drove to the back so she could clear her car out. One by one, she took her time neatly piling the boxes and plastic containers into their new home. When she was done, she secured the unit with a large, metal lock, leaving with nothing except the small, blue tote containing Waleek's cash.

12

———

"Why was Muff leaving here?" Asia asked Waleek's mom, Carolyn, after dropping her purse by the stand near the door and walking to the kitchen. After leaving the storage, she had stopped by Walmart and picked up the items she knew Waleek would need at the city jail. She was just returning from dropping those things off at the jail, along with a money order. She had been through this with Mitch, so she knew exactly how the process worked. She figured she might as well knock everything out before he even had to ask. Her next step was to pay for his lawyer in the morning. When Asia pulled up to the front of their townhouse, she saw Muff pulling out in her dirty-ass Toyota Camry. She wondered who felt they could invite her over without running it by her first. She didn't even have to ask; she knew exactly who it was.

Asia walked into the kitchen where she found Carolyn standing at the sink with a black bonnet on her head. The same bonnet she wore every day around the house. Asia only remembered seeing her with her hair outside of it one time. Carolyn was finishing the last of the dishes and was now tidying up. Her sister Joyce sat at the dining room table. Judging by the smirk on her face, Asia knew something was up. A part of Asia felt like she had walked into an ambush. She stood and waited for Carolyn to reply, but she didn't. She didn't even look up to acknowledge Asia. She instead, continued to spray and wipe down the granite counters around the sink. A small part of Asia felt like Carolyn was miserable. She had one son who her life revolved around and no man. She wasn't an ugly woman. She was a rich shade of chocolate with smooth buttery, blemish-free skin. She was a slim woman; yet she still had a nice shape. Round eyes, full lips; Asia considered her attractive. Her sister Joyce looked nearly identical; except she kept her face in a nasty scowl making her far less attractive.

"Carolyn," Asia said firmly to get her attention. *I know damn well this bitch fuckin' hear me*, she thought to herself. She knew Carolyn didn't like her. She also hoped that she knew the feeling was fucking mutual.

"Why was Muff leaving my house?" Asia continued.

"Yo' house?" Joyce asked, way over from the dining room table. Asia rolled her eyes and went to speak, but Joyce continued. "Carolyn, you better let this bitch know!" Asia already knew shit was about to go left when Joyce entered her home and felt like she could speak to her any kind of way. Waleek hadn't even been gone a full twenty-four hours and they were ready to show their ass. Asia knew this was all about who got first dibs and control to Waleek's money and possessions.

"Asia. First off. This isn't your house. This is *my* shit," Carolyn finally responded casually after neatly placing the rag down on the edge of the counter to dry. Asia could tell by her tone; Carolyn had been wanting to get this off her chest for a while.

Asia glared at Carolyn, her jaws now clenched and her heart pounding. She knew exactly where this was leading to. She knew that Waleek's mother didn't care much for her. It was just never in her best interest to express it to her son, since he was taking care of her. Carolyn stood silently; matching Asia's icy glare.

"Carolyn, with all due respect, when did this become *your* shit?" she asked, glancing over at Joyce. She was waiting for her ass to say something dumb. While it was taking everything in her to keep from snapping on Carolyn, she wouldn't hesitate to lay hands on Joyce's old ass.

"Waleek paid every single bill in here, and he made it very clear to you that this house was for *me*," she clarified. "Now if there's a problem, we can let him sort it out when he calls."

"I don't give a damn about him calling! Waleek's ass ain't getting out no time soon! How the hell you gon' pay the damn rent? You barely work," Carolyn added.

"Haven't since she got with him," Joyce cosigned snidely from the corner.

"You know what! Fuck you!" Asia spat at Joyce, pointing at her. "You always got ya fuckin' mouth in something. Bitch you don't fucking work! I barely work because Waleek don't want me to! Don't nobody say shit about ya broke ass! Every other week you got ya hand out begging him for money!"

"Asia!" Carolyn yelled overtop of her and Joyce, while their arguing increased in volume by the minute. Joyce had even stood up and started walking towards Asia like she wanted to fight her.

"Don't call me!" Asia said wildy. She spun her head around and looked at Carolyn like she'd lost her mind. "Get ya fuckin' sister before I beat her ass!"

"Bitch it'll be a cold day in Hell before you whoop my ass! Red bitch think she can beat me; I'm from North Philly bitch!" she spat, ready to go toe to toe. Her breathing was now heavy, and she was practically jumping up and down, ready to swing.

Carolyn hurried and got in between the two and looked Asia dead in her face.

"You gotta leave Asia," she said, pointing to the door. "You can't stay here with me. My name is on the lease, so I'm asking you to leave."

"You want me to get out of *my own* house?" Asia asked, her eyes widening in disbelief.

"This is *my* house," she emphasized. "You need to leave. And don't come back."

Asia took a deep breath and glared at Carolyn and Joyce. Her eyes were narrowed, and she was trembling from anger. However, she didn't respond. She spun around on her heels and stormed off to pack her belongings.

"I've already cleared your closet and gathered up ya things," Carolyn said.

Asia didn't bother to respond. She headed to the back of the home and stormed into her and Waleek's bedroom. She shook her head in disbelief. Sure enough, all her clothes and shoes had been taken out of the closet and placed into big, black trash bags. *This motherfucking bitch*, she thought. She turned around and walked out to look in Hasan's room. When she got to her son's room, his door was already open, and sure enough, his belongings were packed in garbage bags as well. The sight infuriated her. *To pack up a baby's shit,* she thought angrily. That was all she needed to see. Carolyn could rot in hell for all she cared. She could have the house; she wouldn't keep it long. Her job at the hospital wasn't going to comfortably cover the $3,000 a month rent. Asia had the most important thing to all of them: Waleek's money.

13

"The cops questioned me, but I told them the truth. That I don't know shit," Muff lied into the phone.

Waleek was rambling off question after question and frankly, she was growing irritated. She was from the hood. She knew what the fuck to say to keep a nigga from getting even more jammed up. *If you knew how to control ya fuckin' temper, then you wouldn't be in this mess,* she thought to herself. Of course, she didn't say it, since she knew she was just as at fault as he was. If not more so. Muff had gotten caught playing her usual games, but this time the consequences were dire. She couldn't help but feel an immense amount of guilt. Waleek had killed someone and now her daughter was about to grow up without a father. Even worse, if he didn't leave any money for them, she knew she was ass out. Wasn't nobody kicking out bread to her like Waleek was.

"Listen Waleek, you know my rent due in a week, and I need money for Kayla," Muff said.

She had already been by Waleek's house and met with his mother. She figured Carolyn had the money, so she wasted no time trying to get on her good side so she too would have access to it. Carolyn could be a bitch but usually did as Waleek requested. Waleek had went down for a short bid a few years back when Kayla was a year old, and Carolyn came through on the money-tip. As much money as Waleek was getting in the streets, Muff had no doubt that he had something husky put up. Waleek spent money but he wasn't nearly as flashy as he could have been.

"Can you ask your mom to give me some money, so I can pay it and take care of what I need for your daughter?" she asked. His response would not only surprise her but anger her as well.

"My mom doesn't have my money. Asia does," he said nonchalantly.

"What!" Muff said, becoming immediately angry.

"You remember how she fucked my money up last time. If I can't trust her to do right with a little bit of bread, I damn sure can't trust her to do right with a lot."

Muff smacked her teeth loudly. "Nigga, I could have handled your fuckin' money for all that."

"Yeah fuckin' right Muff. You barely can pay ya bills. Every time I turn around, shit getting cut the fuck off and I gotta pay it."

"Fuck you Waleek! That's the least you can do, especially since I'm pregnant with your fuckin child!" she reminded him.

Waleek sighed heavily through the receiver. He thought that they agreed that she was going to get rid of it. She wasn't even a good mother to Kayla. He certainly didn't want another baby by her. Nevertheless, he was just as much at fault as she was. He always thought with his dick and that's why he was in the situation he was in now.

"Muff just chill out, okay?" he said, doing his best to try and soften her up. He didn't need her running back to Asia with no bullshit. "I'll make sure you get the money for Kayla, the rent, and the abortion you agreed to."

"Abortion!" Muff yelled. "Nigga you got me fucked up! I'm good enough to fuck on, but you don't want any more kids by me! Why? Because of that hi-yellow bitch you got running around living lavish and driving around in a fucking new beamer. You know what ... I got something for yo' ass," she said before hanging up abruptly.

"Fuck!" Waleek yelled out. He shook his head angrily while a few other inmates shot him sympathetic looks. They knew the feeling of frustration all too well since they too went through it regularly.

Waleek glanced up at the clock and realized that count was about to start. Before he could try to call Asia, the C.Os announced that it was count time. He knew he was fucked; especially if Muff got to Asia before he did.

"Now go ask him that! Bitch!" Muff yelled into her phone. She went to yell some more but realized Asia had hung up the phone in her ear. She dialed her number again but realized Asia had blocked her. She'd gotten Asia's new number after Waleek slid through, fucked her, and fell asleep. She always did her best to stay one step ahead of him.

Muff was beyond angry; she was fucking furious. Not only because Asia had hung up on her, but because she couldn't believe that Waleek's blacker than black ass would hand over all his money to a bitch he'd been fucking for less than six months. He didn't even have the decency to put some money to the side for his daughter, or even leave his mother some money just in case she needed something. Instead, Asia had access to every fucking penny belonging to him, meaning she could delegate it how she saw fit, regardless of what Waleek wanted. Muff knew Asia wasn't going to give her a dime, especially since the last time they'd saw each other, they'd come to blows. It also didn't help that every opportunity she got, she would taunt Asia, just like she'd done less than a minute ago until she hung up on her.

Muff slammed her fist into the palm of her opposite hand. She hated that things had played out so terribly. Zee was dead and Waleek was sitting in jail because of it. Waleek's stupid ass knew they had cameras all over the complex. His face was plastered all over the video clear as day. That's what had gotten him booked; she was hoping that would also get him off. Zee and the two other guys with him had jumped on Waleek and chased him down. He'd acted purely in self-defense. Any juror would be able to see that. The only problem for Muff was Waleek didn't know that she had helped identify him.

What Muff failed to disclose to Waleek was that she too was on the video and had been identified. She was one of the first people that was picked up and questioned. While her mama and aunt sat in the lobby of the city precinct, Muff was being questioned in the back. She told them everything that happened just like her mama told her too. She told them that Waleek was just defending himself; yet, they still locked him up and charged him with murder. Muff didn't think that Waleek would try to harm her in any way, but she could never be too sure. Growing up in the city of Philadelphia, she'd seen men turn on their own siblings and kill their own mama's when shit hit the fan. She hoped Waleek got off on the charges before she's forced to testify. *Fuck that, I'm not going to testify*, she thought to herself. Whatever happened, she just hoped Waleek didn't find out that she'd opened her mouth and ratted him out.

14

———

"Fuck you Waleek!" Asia spat, clenching the phone tightly. "Muff told me what the fuck it is! She told me the *real* story of what happened! So, you can miss me with the bullshit."

Asia had waited up for hours for Waleek's phone call. She couldn't wait to tell him that she was done with his ass. Before the cuffs were tight on his wrists, Muff wasted no time spilling the beans about what happened. She also made sure to rub it in Asia's face that they were still fucking and had never stopped, even though she had come into the picture. Everything he'd told Asia had been a big ass lie.

"Babe please! Listen to me," he begged, damn near in tears. *Please don't do this right now. I need you,* he thought to himself.

Waleek knew he had fucked up, but he couldn't lose Asia right now. He needed her. In reality, he needed everyone he could get in his corner. He gripped the phone tightly with one hand and used the other to rub his head in frustration. He glanced around the tier quickly to see if there were any nigga's close by that were listening. He didn't want anyone seeing him begging on the phone to a bitch, since that was exactly what he was about to do.

"No! I'm not listening to shit! I've heard enough of your lies. You been gone two fucking days and everybody's true colors have shown. Fuck you! Fuck Muff! And fuck ya mother!" she spat.

Waleek sat quietly on the phone in pure disbelief. He couldn't believe Asia was being so disrespectful. After everything he'd done for her.

"Baby please. If you let me explain." If she would just let him talk. If she would just hear him out.

"What's there to explain Waleek? The bitch is pregnant, and you've been lying to me! I know everything! Every fucking thing!" she screamed with tears in her eyes. She hated the pain she felt. She hated that her heart was being weighed down once again by an ungrateful ass nigga.

"I know about the house that bitch has in the county! The one you just got her! I know about the baby she's carrying! And I also know that ya bitch ass mother don't fuck with me!"

"Woah! Woah! Asia! Chill the fuck out," Waleek demanded. She was going way too far left. He knew his mother wasn't Asia's biggest fan, but she'd never been disrespectful to her. She'd always been cordial and shown Asia respect.

Asia's disrespect for his mother made him feel like she was trying to get out on him because he was now weak and vulnerable. He hated that he had put himself in such a position to even have to endure that type of treatment. This was the same bitch he'd basically took in while she was homeless. He'd put her out in the sticks; had her sitting pretty while whipping a foreign; put thousands of dollars in her pocket. And this was the thanks he got! *This bitch got me all the way fucked up*, he thought to himself angrily.

"Fuck you Waleek! Ya mother had my shit packed and bagged up when I got back from taking care of shit for you! You hadn't even been gone twenty-four-hours! So, fuck that! You chill the fuck out! I'm back at a fuckin' hotel with my fucking son. I have nowhere to go. So, fuck that shit you talking," she cried.

The reality of her situation was truly setting in. "She had your fucking baby-mother in our house when I was gone! When I pulled up, Muff was leaving my fuckin' house. After all the disrespect this bitch has directed towards me! And *then,* to top it off, she had my shit packed up ... And then proceeded to tell me, *this ain't yo' shit! This my shit! My name is on the lease.* So, I gotta get the fuck out!" she said screaming wildly.

"Me and my son have nowhere to go!" she continued to emphasize. Waleek had promised her. He knew how she felt about not being stable for Hasan.

"I can't go back to my mother's house and you fuckin' know that! I'm back to square fucking one!" she screamed into the receiver.

Waleek knew everything that she had been through. He had promised her that no one would ever be able to kick her back out on the streets ever again. But look at her now; homeless again. When Waleek told her that his mom had to go on the lease she didn't dispute it. She figured she was just doing it to make things easier for him. How wrong she was! As soon as the papers were signed, Waleek informed her that Carolyn would also be staying there. Although Asia protested, her pleas fell on deaf ears. Waleek argued that he couldn't tell her no since she too had signed the lease to help get them the house. Asia knew Carolyn was up to something, but she never again spoke on it. Now she knew what the "something" was.

Before Waleek could respond to the last thing Asia said, she hung up. She didn't want to hear anything else he had to say. She was done. She had enough on her plate dealing with Mitch's weekly phone calls from the prison; she wasn't about to incorporate Waleek's into her life as well. One thing about

Mitch was, he was a solid nigga. He took care of Asia when he was home and never let any of his street dealings slip into their home. Waleek was out of pocket and the only way to deal with him, was to cut him off. The call she had just terminated, would be the last one she ever took.

Asia threw her phone into the seat next to her, buried her head into her hands and began to sob. *Why me*, she asked herself; however, she already knew why. Asia knew her most critical flaw was her dependency. First it was Mitch, then her mom, then Waleek. She had to stop depending on people! And stop it immediately. She wiped the tears away from her wet face with the sleeve of her shirt. She was done crying, and she was tired of being a weak bitch. She was determined to rise. She had a son to provide for. Asia knew that she was no longer going to be able to just wing it through life. Her next step was to formulate a plan.

WALEEK PACED BACK in forth in his cell. He was stressed to the point he felt sick. He hadn't eaten all day and he barely could think straight. He had been calling Asia non-stop and she wasn't answering. He had fucked up. Not only was he facing a murder charge, but the person closest to him was talking about leaving him. He hadn't come to grips with the reality that Asia was done. He wouldn't allow himself to accept it. He prayed she didn't leave. She had all his money and he needed her. He was at one of the worst points he'd ever been.

Waleek knew that he was getting what his hand had called. He should have been stopped dealing with Muff; however, he always thought with his dick. *Look where the fuck this shit got me,* he thought. After pacing the small cell, Waleek sat down on the hard bunk. He hoped he was able to get out of this one. Last time, he gave up a name, but this time, there was no name to give up but his own. He'd acted in self-defense. He either had to prove that, or say it wasn't him and he was never there. With witnesses there, he didn't want to take that route, especially since the prosecutor and police could easily coerce someone into pointing the finger at him in a courtroom. Self-defense was his only option. Even if Asia did leave him, he prayed she did right by him and payed for his lawyer. For the first time, he needed her, and it wasn't the other way around.

15

THREE MONTHS LATER

"I already gave his lawyer $25,000 and I sat aside another $25,000, just in case they want more."

"Yeah, that's about right. In case he decides to take it to trial. You don't want to shit on the nigga completely. You deserve part of that money since he put you through hella shit," Mitch cosigned. "Plus, you never want to play with a nigga freedom. He a hustler; he gon make that money back ten-fold. But don't play games with the lawyer fees. Stay solid on that," Mitch schooled her.

"Yeah, that'll be taken care of," she assured him.

After being put out of her home and arguing with Muff, she decided to call it quits with Waleek. She dealt with enough shit. Even though she knew that Waleek was cheating, the financial security he provided, kept her with him. Once Muff revealed that she was pregnant and that Waleek had gotten booked because he killed a nigga that she was fucking, she decided enough was enough. Asia booked her a room at the extended stay in Willow Grove and had been there since. It had been nearly a month and she was still there. Initially, she was heartbroken. Not only did she have to deal with Waleek being gone and possibly facing a life sentence, she also had to deal with the fact that he cheated on her and got someone else pregnant. His baby-mother out of all people. A bitch that had threatened her, antagonized her, and jumped on her. She hated to leave him at his lowest point, but she had no choice. The disrespect was out of control.

She knew that everybody and they mama was going to have something to say, but she didn't give a damn. She was the one that had to put up with his constant disrespect. After checking into her suite with her son, Asia went through the tote containing Waleek's money. He had $250k saved up. Asia knew that he would need a lawyer. She was about to do him dirty, but she wasn't going to do him too dirty. That Monday morning, she called up the lawyer he requested and dropped $25,000 on his case. Since it was a murder case, she put another $25,000 to the side. She rode back down to Bala Cynwyd when his mother was gone and left him another $100k in his car. The final $100k, was hers. She was keeping it because she deserved it. She didn't care who disputed that fact.

"So, how things going with starting the business?" Mitch asked, breaking Asia away from her thoughts.

"It's going good!" Asia said happily. "My boss been schooling me on everything that I need, so it's going good. Although I don't have a degree, she's going to sign on as a director. That way, on paper I'm fully in compliance but everything will still be mine. I'll pay her monthly of course, to help me oversee things and make sure I'm running according to the state guidelines. I already have the building and I just hired four girls. I'm excited," she admitted.

"That's wassup. I knew you had it in you. I knew that you would make something out of yourself and build something for our son," he said proudly.

"Thanks Mitch," she said, smiling at the unexpected compliment. While she wasn't necessarily proud of the way she obtained the money, she *was* proud of the way that she was investing it. She wanted more out of her life. She wanted more for her son's life. She wanted him as far away from the hood as possible. Even if she had to continue paying the $2,000 a month for her extended stay; she wasn't going back to the hood.

After Waleek got booked, Asia had to sit down and really evaluate herself and what she wanted to do with her life. She was nearly twenty-two years old and didn't have shit. Instead of being on top of her game and working towards a goal like a real mother and woman would be doing; she was going through hella degrading shit to keep a roof over her head and keep a nigga taking care of her. She decided then that it would be the last time she was like that. She decided that even if a nigga took care of her, she would also be able to take care of herself. Instead of ripping and running the streets, she immersed herself in work and learning the daycare business. She had even signed up for a couple online child-care classes at the community college. She began focusing her energy on positive shit. If it wasn't making her better or contributing to her goals, she refused to make time for it. Within a couple of months, she had met the right people and began putting her plan for a daycare in motion.

Asia sat on the couch and looked at the microwave. It was nine o'clock a.m. She had to get going. She sat up from her reclined position and got up. "Look, I'm about to get going. I'm having some furniture delivered and I have some guys coming in today to start painting. I'm meeting them at ten-thirty."

"Cool. I'm gon' let you go handle yo' business. Oh!" Mitch exclaimed. He had almost forgot. "I want to run something by you later today. I know you've been spending a lot of money on this new business. Since I'm here, I haven't been able to help you with that. Til now. I'll run shit by you later tonight when I call back."

"Okay," Asia said. She had walked into the bathroom and was now applying a thin coat of nude gloss to her lips.

After saying goodbye, she ended the call with Mitch and went back out into the rest of the open suite to wake her son up. She looked at him sleep peacefully. Everything she did, was for him. She just wanted him to have a good life. The daycare she was opening was hopefully the beginning of one. Although it was a good start for someone like her, she knew that she was going to have to continue investing in order to live like she really wanted to. Between the hotel they were living in, car maintenance, repairs and insurance, and the daycare startup fees, she was down nearly $30,000 already. She had about seventy left. Her daycare was going to be in the Mt. Airy section of Philadelphia. Although that area consisted of middle-class residents, she knew that most of her parents were going to be paying with state provided funds. According to her former boss and mentor, that could take sixty to ninety days to come through. Because of that, she knew she was going to need to set aside around $30,000 to pay her staff for the first three months. She prayed things worked out. Starting a business was necessary; however, it was a scary process because she had to lose so much money in the beginning.

Asia woke Hasan, got him dressed, and headed out. Her daycare was on a busy section of Wadsworth Avenue, right before you got to Cheltenham Avenue. To her, the location was perfect. She was still able to serve the black community; however, the black people she served had a little more class. If she'd got a building in North Philly, most of the parents would have been young and ghetto. Additionally, they were notorious for not holding jobs long. For her business to be successful, she had to have consistent enrollment and attendance. She knew that would be easier to achieve with the location she had chosen. So far, she didn't have any regrets. She had already had parents inquiring about the location and had even given out a few applications for slots.

Asia's day ran smoothly. The painters did a beautiful job on the walls; taking them from an off-white to a light gray. She also killed time by riding over to the nearby Walmart at Cedarbrook mall to pick up toys, supplies, and decorations. She smiled when she was nearly finished. Hasan hobbled around happily like he was in Heaven. He was part of the reason she had chosen to open a daycare. She wanted to run a business that incorporated her son. She didn't need a sitter since she could take him right to work with her. He'd also be learning and developing social skills why he was there. She was going to do everything in her power to break generational curses and make sure he grew up to be a well-rounded young man.

Although Mitch felt he was useless because he couldn't help her financially; to Asia, his contribution was monumental. He gave her tons of ideas and encouraged her daily. Since Waleek went to jail, their relationship had strengthened immensely. She vowed that no one would ever again come between their friendship. She wondered what he needed to run by her. Whatever it was; she knew that she would probably go along with it. His role in her life was unmatched and she trusted him with her life.

MITCH WALKED out into the visiting room and smiled warmly at his former cell-buddy Josiah. He'd met him in the city jail a year ago and they became fast friends. Mitch saw something in Josiah that Josiah also saw in Mitch: hustle. Josiah was a few years older than he was and was considered King-Pin status out in his hometown of Delaware. He had gotten jammed up transporting drugs into Philadelphia. Because of the large amount of drugs he had been caught with, Josiah was held without bond.

After a year and a half of fighting, he was acquitted because of an illegal search.

Talking to Josiah daily, Mitch learned that he was very intelligent. He decided that if he ever had the opportunity to do business with him, he would. Real recognized real, and he had no doubt that Josiah was a solid nigga.

"Wassup, big man!" Mitch said, grinning wildly as he shook hands with Josiah. Big man was a nickname Mitch had given him because of his large stature. Josiah stood in at six foot three and weighed around 250-pounds. However, not an ounce of it was fat. Josiah was fit and solid. He resembled a quarterback football player.

"Wassup, Mitchie Mitch," he replied, embracing his friend. Although they hadn't known each other long, they were truly quite fond of one another. In the drug game, it was rare to come across solid individuals.

For the first five minutes they played catch up. Josiah asked about Mitch's family, while Mitch inquired about Josiah's mother. He remembered that her health had at one point been failing, while Josiah was locked up awaiting trial.

"Mama's good, man! She down in Florida with my sister and her kids. She's living it the fuck up," he laughed. "You know how Mama do. She lives like she a queen."

"Only right," Mitch said. "She birthed a king," Mitch said, referring to his King Pin status.

"You already know. But check this out. I'm trying to get you where you need to be as well. To make sure your family is good," Josiah stated, his handsome face becoming serious.

"That's what I'm talkin' bout. That's what I'm tryin' to hear," Mitch nodded, leaning in closer to Josiah so he could inform him on what the new move involved.

16

Asia stood outside of Sweet Treats Desserts and looked around like she was lost. She was puzzled that Mitch's friend had chosen that spot for them to meet at. There was no one out front, and after glancing inside of the shop, there was nowhere to sit. She assumed they would be meeting at a restaurant. She prayed he hurried. It was mid-June and it was hot as Hell outside. Fanning herself with her hand, she used the other to dig in her leather tote and scrounge around until she found her phone. After pulling up the message, she realized she was at the correct spot.

"Asia?" someone called out.

Asia turned around and had to look up. She was only five-three, but the man in front of her had to be nearly a foot taller.

"How you doing?" he asked smoothly, extending his hand to introduce himself. "I'm Josiah. Mitch's homie."

"Hi," she said with a toothy grin. Josiah's presence had her hot. She was instantly attracted to him. Mitch was fine; but Josiah was *lawd have mercy* fine. He was that fucking fine. Tall with toasty brown skin, he looked like he could be the rapper Dave East's big brother.

"I'm ugh A-A Asia," she stuttered.

"What chu nervous for. I ain't gon kidnap you," he said. *Shit, I wouldn't mind if you did,* Asia thought. She had to give him credit; he was charming without even trying. However, she had come there for Mitch, so she was about to cut out all the bull-shit and get down to business.

"Come on," he waved, walking ahead of her into the bakery. "I just had lunch and I always get a sweet-tooth right after," he laughed.

"Me too," she grinned. She thought she was the only one.

Josiah held the door and Asia walked ahead of him and into the bakery. The smell of fresh bread wafted through the air, along with the heavenly smell of cinnamon, strawberry, and vanilla. She was never going to lose any weight with this kind of temptation.

"How are you two doing?" the clerk asked from the counter. "Take your time to check out the selection. Let me know if you have any questions or when you're ready to order."

"Thank you," they both responded politely.

As Asia looked through the glass display case at the delightful assortment of pastries and cakes, Josiah came beside her and looked as well. He didn't need to; he was familiar with every item they sold, since he owned the place. It was custom for the clerk to greet him like he was any other customer, no matter how often he came in.

"So, did Mitch go over what you needed to bring?" he asked in a low voice as he stood beside her.

"Yeah," she replied. She'd brought the $20,000 like Mitch had requested. She prayed this wasn't a shady deal. With Mitch being in jail, if things went wrong, she would be the one taking the loss. Nevertheless, Mitch reassured her that Josiah was a stand-up guy.

"What exactly are we doing?" she continued. Before she put her cash in anyone's hands, she needed to know what was going on. She knew how Mitch got down, so she didn't expect to be completely filled in; however, if she was going to hand over a dime, she needed to be briefed.

"Let's just say …transporting is big business. Yo' man works in the kitchen at the prison. He assists the C.O with receiving goods into the facility. Goods like industrial size can-goods, macaroni boxes …Shit like that. Everything's packaged up in boxes. The product will be inside."

"But doesn't that put Mitch at risk?" she asked.

"Of course, it does. There's always risk in the game. Just like on the street, work moves in the prison system. Him working closely by the kitchen and prison warehouse gives him an opportunity many other inmates won't have. Once I wave my hand, a bulk of that prisons work will come to, and belong to him. I deliver and Mitch will work out all the jailhouse shit. So, that's what you're paying for."

Josiah glanced at Asia to make sure she was following him. Initially he was against giving her so much information. However, with Mitch's persistence, he was instructed to fill her in.

"Mitch wanted to start off big because there's so much money to be made inside," he continued noticing she seemed to be absorbing all the information he was giving her. "Once all the drugs are sold, I'll have someone on the outside, collecting the money that was made on the inside. Once I pick it up, I'll deliver it back to you. Because product is so hard to get in and so scarce in the prison system; Mitch can quadruple his profit in a month. I'll take your $20,000 today and probably bring you back," he paused to do a quick calculation. "He'll make at least $80,000. You'll get your $20,000 back, pocket $40,000 and of course, it'll take another $20,000 for Mitch to get a new package. For you, the first month is what you'll feel is the riskiest. After that, you'll have $60,000 in pure profit."

Damn, that's crazy, Asia thought. She didn't realize prison drug profits were so large. Although the move was insanely profitable, she didn't want Mitch to get into trouble. However, at the end of the day, Mitch was a grown man that called his own shots. The sixty-thousand-dollars a month would help tremendously. The more she thought about it; in order to give her son the life she wanted him to have, she needed it.

"Okay," she said. Asia went to dig in her bag to get the stack of hundreds that were neatly wrapped inside.

"Nah," he laughed. "I'll come to you and get it. I'll always pick it up from you. Makes it easier."

"Okay." She zipped her bag back up and prepared to leave.

"Where you going?" he asked. "You forgot to order something."

"Ummm. I'm not really hungry. But the cherry, cream-cheese Danish looks good," she said.

"Okay ... Good choice," he said, giving Asia a quick head to toe scan. It was the first time she had turned around and faced him completely. He had to admit, she was gorgeous. Her large eyes and full lips gave her an exotic look, while her skin was a beautiful rich shade of light brown. He could tell that the sun had darkened it.

"We're ready to order," he said to the clerk. He pointed to the pastry that Asia had chosen. "Let me get uuhhh ... ten dozen," he said.

"Ten dozen?" Asia asked, her already wide eyes, widening to the size of saucers. "I can't eat that many Danishes," she laughed.

"I know. I don't expect you to. I'm going to have them delivered to your center ... For the kids," he smiled. "I'll pick up the money then. Moving forward, I'll send you an order every month. It'll come in a bakery truck. You'll sign an invoice and hand over $20,000 in cash to the driver."

Suddenly, it all made more sense. Asia now knew exactly how things were going to work. Although the move Mitch was trying to make seemed elaborate and a little tedious, she knew that if he had his hands in it, it was going to work. Mitch was a hustler and from what she gathered, so was Josiah.

LATER THAT EVENING, Josiah stood alone, staring out the window of his spacious, condo in downtown Wilmington. It was on the twentieth floor and overlooked the Delaware river. He had purchased it specifically for the view, so every chance he got, he would stand there and admire it. He looked down at the water. The light from the skyline sparkled and glistened off it. It was truly breathtaking.

Josiah had purchased the spot about a year ago; however, he didn't spend much time in it. Instead, he flew back and forth to Florida to be with his sister, mother, and nieces. Josiah swirled around his short glass of cognac before he took a hard sip from it. Ignoring the burn the alcohol produced, his mind drifted to Asia. Something about her had him drawn to her. And it was more than just her beauty. He didn't know if it was her sunny disposition or her beautiful smile. Or maybe it was the way Mitch used to talk about her during their nights in the city jail. He always spoke highly of her. He knew at one point; she was his queen. Unfortunately, with twenty to thirty years above his head, Mitch knew that he would have to one day allow his queen to find a new king. Josiah quickly shook the thoughts.

Josiah contributed his interest to the fact that he was pushing thirty and was ready to settle down. At twenty-nine years old, he expected his life to be a little different. Instead of standing alone in a four-bedroom condo, he should be hearing the sweet voice of his wife throughout. He should hear the pitter patter of tiny feet running about. The smell of spaghetti sauce and pasta wafting in the air. Or, maybe the light bark of a tiny, little dog named Fido. Josiah laughed to himself at the name. *Fido. Nah, maybe something different.* Josiah did however want every single one of those things. He was ready for a family. He wasn't ashamed to admit that he was lonely. He had a whole lot of money and no one to share it with except his mother and sister. He had his nieces whom he loved dearly. They were twins and every time he saw them; it was a painful reminder that he wanted children of his own. He refused to rush things. He was ready but he wasn't desperate.

He'd had his fair share of women; however, none of them had ever been worthy of settling down with. Most of them were crazy, or simply nothing more than gold-diggers. He also needed someone who already understood the game. He needed someone who knew a whole lot about loyalty. Josiah was a firm believer of fate. Something told him that fate had led him to Asia. He wasn't exactly sure how he would play a role in her life, or vice versa, but he wanted to find out. He decided that he would try his hand. He wanted to at least get to know her ... and then let the chips fall where they may.

17

———

"How you doing?" Josiah asked while displaying a confident smile. He had just walked into Asia's daycare and was looking around in awe. The place looked good. It didn't look like the typical daycare center. Asia had a beautiful "under the sea," water theme going that you didn't see too often. As soon as you walked in there was a seating area with approximately six chairs. Separating the seating area from the center was a large desk that spanned across the front. A small door led behind the desk.

"Hi!" Asia smiled while approaching from out the back room where her office was. Her building had state-of-the-art cameras, so she saw when Josiah's bakery van pulled up to make its very first delivery. She almost didn't recognize who he was, until he stepped out and faced the camera. The first time she'd met him he was dressed casually; today he had on tan khaki shorts and a white, short-sleeved Polo shirt. Asia noticed the tattoos on his strong, defined arms. He looked handsome and very polished; although still sexy as hell.

"How was your drive?" she asked, as if they were old friends and she'd known him for years. A part of her was happy to see him again. She stood behind the desk while Josiah still stood in the seating area close by the door.

"The drive was good," he nodded. "I like what you've done with the place," he said, looking around again.

"Thank you. I wanted something different for the kids. Something fun," she said, turning her head from side to side and glancing at her own creation.

"Well, you did a good job," he complimented. Josiah stared at her for a second and went to say something, but for some weird reason he was at a loss for words.

Asia looked at him weirdly and then laughed. "Something wrong?" she asked.

Josiah grinned nervously. "Nah ... I just forgot what the hell I was about to say," he said. "Looking at you," he admitted.

He paused for a second. He hated to make her feel uncomfortable, but she was truly beautiful. The last time he saw her, she had her hair down, but today it was up in a messy ponytail and she was stunning. He noticed she had a small mole on the side of her neck. He had an urge to kiss it. *What the fuck is wrong with you, nigga,* he thought to himself. Mitch was his friend. He had sent him to handle business, not fuck his girl.

Noticing Josiah acting a little strangely, Asia decided to lead their conversation. "So, where's the delivery?" she asked.

"Oh, shit. I almost forgot. I gotta go grab it."

He walked out of the daycare and opened the back doors of the delivery van. When he returned inside, he had ten boxes of Danishes stacked on top of one another.

Asia couldn't believe he could carry all ten boxes, but then she realized he had long arms. She glanced at him and couldn't help but wonder what else on him was long.

"You can bring them back here," Asia said. She opened the door and Josiah walked through carrying the boxes. After letting the door close, she proceeded to lead him back into the small kitchen. It was small, but it had all the necessary equipment to prepare meals and store them.

Josiah stacked the boxes on the counter while Asia excused herself for a few minutes. She went to her office and retrieved the $20,000 he was also scheduled to pick up. While she was away, he looked around and noticed the center was impeccably clean. The faint scent of bleach lingered in the air. He loved a clean woman.

"Here you go," she said smiling brightly. "Twenty thousand." The bills were neatly separated by thin paper sleeves. He could tell that they had come from the bank that way.

"Thanks," Josiah said solemnly, accepting the money and placing it into the large fanny pack his drivers carried to store cash.

Josiah's solemn tone was unintentional, but that was the way he felt. He hated to leave. As much as he knew he shouldn't, he liked Asia. His hectic schedule and lifestyle didn't make it possible for him to have a decent love life. When he did meet someone, he'd soon learn that they were only there for the money. Asia seemed different. She seemed to know money. Well, not the kind he had, but nevertheless, she seemed to know money. Asia was no longer destitute and broke, so she wasn't looking specifically for a nigga that would take care of her. He liked that. He needed to be around somcone who didn't need him. He wanted to find out everything about her; truly get to know her.

"So, what time do you close up shop?" he asked. He figured he might as well try his hand. She could either say yes or no.

"Ummm ... Probably around six. I have a little paperwork to do, so I'll be here a little later than usual."

"Oh okay ... Cool. I have a few more deliveries to make around here so I'll be in the city until then," he lied.

Picking up the money was the only reason he had drove into Philadelphia. There were no other deliveries. The truck was nothing more than a front in case he got pulled over by the police. The goal was the look like a legitimate worker at a legitimate company.

"You know any good places to eat?" he asked.

"Umm. Not too many around here, but there is this little Italian restaurant you could check out in Manayunk. I stumbled upon it by accident one day," she said. She remembered running across the place when she lived in Bala Cynwyd. Manayunk was no more than a ten-minute drive away.

"You want to come with me ... Show me?" he asked.

He felt like he damn near wanted to choke after getting the words out. He sucked at shooting his shot. As much money as he had; he wished he had some game to go with it.

"I can't," she said sadly. "I have my son with me. I can't ask anyone to watch him at the last minute. Especially not at that hour."

Although disappointed, Josiah respected it. He admired the fact that she said no so easily; placing her son's needs before anything and anyone.

"Well, you can bring him ... If you want," Josiah said. He wasn't giving up that easy.

Asia looked at Josiah and smiled warmly. She could tell he liked her, and she admired his tasteful persistence. "Okay," she said with surprise. "I'll bring him."

"Yeah?" he asked, a little surprised, but happy that she agreed.

"Yeah. He won't mind the meal, and he'll be nice and full by the time I get home. That makes life easier for me," she admitted.

"Cool. So, I'll pick you up from here at six?" he asked.

"In the delivery van?" she asked with a laugh. She looked outside to the van and back at him.

"Oh shit. I almost forgot I was in it. Well, how about, I *meet* you here and you drive?"

"Sounds like a plan."

ASIA AND JOSIAH dined at a restaurant called Mama Bella's. It was a quaint little restaurant on a busy street in the heart of Manayunk. They chatted lightly, while Hasan made a mess in his hi-chair. All three of them ordered Chicken Fettuccini Alfredo. Both were fans of soul food and didn't know much about Italian. They figured they would stay on the safe side, so they didn't order something they didn't like.

As they ate and talked about random things, Josiah hesitated to ask Asia all the questions he really wanted to know. That of course, was until they both ordered a glass of wine. The drop of liquid courage that penetrated Josiah's system allowed him to ask the questions he really wanted to know.

"So, how long have you and Mitch been together? How did you two meet?" he finally asked.

"We met at a Chinese store," she laughed. She thought it was funny how they met, especially because she truly had made the first move to spark up conversation.

"I had taken the bus to South West Philly to see my girlfriend down there. We got hungry, so we stopped to get some chicken wings. Mitch rolled up in this ugly ass jeep. It was new and I could tell it was expensive, but it was hideous. Me and my homegirl walked out, and there he was, doing his best to look extra cool. Me being young and sassy; I come out and tell him, you're cute but that jeep is ugly as hell. He had no choice but to respond. He made a move; we became inseparable and the rest is history," she laughed again, thinking back to the day they met. "And technically, we aren't together," she continued. "Haven't been in over a year," she said. She used a napkin and wiped the ring of food from around Hasan's mouth. He squirmed and turned his head in protest.

"How come? If you don't mind me asking."

"Well, as you probably already know, Mitch got a pretty big sentence. Twenty to thirty years in prison. It just wasn't realistic for him to ask me to wait or put my life on hold. At first, I wasn't feeling it. I felt like I would be turning my back on him. However, he told me he wanted me to live my life, so I eventually agreed."

"Damn. I understand though. It's only right. Only fair," he nodded, before picking up his water glass and taking a small sip. "So, you've just been chilling since Mitch been down?" Josiah asked.

Asia realized where the conversation was headed. She liked Josiah. He was tall, handsome, and his presence just screamed power, although he didn't seem to care to advertise it. She found herself attracted to him; however, he was Mitch's friend. She didn't know if that was a boundary, she was willing to cross.

"At first, I was riding solo. I wasn't interested in anyone. My son was only one and I had to deal with the fact that my baby father had damn near got a life sentence. Mitch didn't leave me any money. He didn't trust me to handle it, and I get it. He left it to his mom, and she blew through it. She got him a shitty ass lawyer and spent what was left. Don't get me wrong, I love her, and I know there was no malice behind it, but she's from the hood and hood people blow through money when they get a lump sum. That's exactly what she did. So, I'm out here, and didn't have shit except a baby to support. No money, no car, no crib. I moved in with my mother and she treated me and my baby like shit, while my little brother stole from me. To the point where I had nothing left."

"Damn," Josiah said. His heart went out to her for what she had went through. He wished he could just tell her that he had the ability to fix all that. Make sure she never went through anything like that again. However, he was sure she had heard it all before, and didn't believe it; nor wanted to hear it again.

"So, to make a long story short. I wound up running into a nigga that took me out the hood, got me on my feet, but at the end of the day, fucked me over emotionally."

"How'd he manage to do that?" Josiah asked, prying even more.

Asia stopped for a minute and burst into laughter. "Damn nigga! What you the Feds? You ask a million questions!" she continued to laugh lightheartedly. She reached around and gave him a playful nudge.

"Nah ... I'm just trying to figure you out. Understand you," he smiled.

"Understand me for what, though?" she asked. She took her arms and folded them across her chest. "What do you want to understand me for?"

"Because I want to get to know you. I'd like to know what makes you happy. What makes you smile. What makes you angry. I'd like to know what makes your life hard ... And how I can make it all easier for you. I'd like to spend some time with you. Really get to know you," he admitted. He glanced at Hasan. "And your son. If that's okay with you."

Josiah figured he would just lay it all on the line. He didn't have time for games. He'd gotten this far, and he didn't want to go back to Delaware without knowing whether he had a chance.

"I don't know if that's appropriate," she said quietly. She too was shocked that Josiah had been so blunt about his intentions.

"As a man, I don't think Mitch will have a problem with it. If that's what your insinuating. I'm a real nigga. I take care of those I love, and I do right by those I love. I have no doubt in my mind that you and your son could easily fall into that category."

Asia sat quietly and thought about what he said. A part of her hated to start over. Waleek had done her so wrong and she just wanted to give her heart time to heal.

"I don't know," she muttered quietly. "I've been hurt. Hurt by Mitch leaving, and then hurt by the last nigga dogging and deceiving me. I don't know if I'm ready to give my heart to someone again that quickly."

"I'm not asking for your heart though. Not right away, anyway. All I'm asking is for your time. If you give me your time, there's no pressure. I just want to spend some time with you," he said honestly.

"Okay," Asia said reluctantly.

Her response caused Josiah to light up. He had no doubt that she would be his. He just hoped that Mitch was truly okay with it like he said he would be. Regardless of the fact, that it was someone he considered his friend.

18

Mitch stood in the warehouse that sat behind the kitchen area. It was way to the back of the prison so one wouldn't notice it when coming to visit. When he was assigned a work activity, he had initially started working in the kitchen. However, after displaying a stellar performance, he was able to transfer to the warehouse once a position opened. Initially he was happy and content with the position. Working in the warehouse payed more than the other prison jobs available for the inmates. He made around eighty dollars a month and was able to pay for his own commissary and hygiene products. He didn't like bothering Asia for anything. He knew being in prison was his own fault and he wasn't about to make anyone suffer with him. After his mom blew through his money, he vowed that when the opportunity arose, he would make some moves to make some real money.

Although Waleek had been taking care of Asia and Hasan, he still saw them as *his* family. He wasn't one to come in the way of her livelihood or her bread, so he remained quiet. However, when the first opportunity came, he jumped in Asia's ear to make sure she would never need another nigga other than him.

He was the one who encouraged her to take half of Waleek's money. He also was the one that convinced her to limit her trips to the city, as well as open her business outside of the city. Mitch knew niggas and was well connected, so he wasn't particularly worried about her safety. Besides, he had asked around, and he learned that Waleek seemed to love Asia. He doubted he would do anything to try and harm her. Regardless of the fact, Mitch kept his ears to the street and had someone following Waleek's court case closely.

Mitch wiped the sweat off his forehead and waited for the delivery truck to come. "It's hot as shit in here," he complained. He used the back of his hand to wipe sweat away from his forehead.

"Should be used to it by now nigga. You work in the heat every day," the C.O sarcastically replied.

"Shut the fuck up," Mitch said annoyed. He cut his eyes at him. He could tell the officer was also hot. He had dug in his pants pocket and pulled out his handkerchief. He used it to wipe the sweat off his face.

Even though the officer got on his nerves, Mitch was thankful that he had ran into him. The C.O was also from Philly but had moved in the sticks to take a job as a warehouse supervisor in the prison. Officer Kelly was as crooked as the letter J. In Mitch's opinion, he should damn near be ready to retire since he made so much money helping inmates smuggle drugs in and out of the prison.

Once Mitch stumbled upon the operation, he swooped in and took it over. He had to knock a couple of people over, but because it was lucrative, he decided he didn't have a choice. Before Mitch took over, there was an older Spanish guy smuggling the bulk of the drugs in. The rumor was, he also used them too. They'd found him dead in his cell a few months ago from an overdose. Although they didn't suspect foul play, a few people truly knew what happened to him. With Marco dead and gone, his position in the warehouse became available. Already acquainted with Officer Kelly, he pulled him to the side and pitched his game plan. Officer Kelly had two children in college, a large mortgage, and a wife that liked to shop. It didn't take much to convince him to take the extra $10,000 a month.

"Here they come now," Officer Kelly said.

The large tractor trailer with Delta Food on the side of it, approached the warehouse at a slow and steady pace. After driving down the long winding path for a minute, the truck pulled to the ramp and slowed for a stop. Mitch smiled. Josiah was the man. He didn't know how he managed to get all the drugs on the truck, but he damn sure got it done. He didn't know if he paid the driver or someone on the inside, but for the past few months, Josiah made sure his package was delivered like clockwork.

The driver, a white man in his forties, got out of the truck with his clipboard and paperwork. The delivery was no-touch freight, so he didn't have to move a thing. Mitch and Officer Kelly would have to unload it. Most of the trucks that came through were no touch freight. The driver handed the paperwork and clipboard over to Officer Kelly so he could sign it. On the sheet was the details of the delivery. After he signed, the driver unhooked the latch and pushed up the gate so they could begin unloading.

Mitch climbed aboard the back and begin pulling the boxes out. Each box he grabbed, he would hand down to Officer Kelly to stack on a dolly and wheel back inside. Once the truck was unloaded, they would place the boxes in a small storage room. The warehouse only had one shift, so they weren't worried about anyone touching the boxes. Officer Kelly was the only one other than Mitch that had access to it. There were a few other guys in the kitchen that would smuggle drugs back to their tier. Mitch also had a couple of inmates who worked in cleaning. They would also help smuggle drugs to other parts of the jail or to other cleaners. Selling drugs in the prison was extremely profitable, albeit risky. The same rules on the street, applied inside as well.

In order to maintain operations and keep from getting caught, Mitch had to make sure he dealt with individuals who were loyal and wouldn't tell. He also had to have several guards on his payroll; greasing their palm so they would look the other way. The move worked out for Mitch in all aspects. He was able to spend as much money as he needed to begin fighting for an appeal, and he was able to take care of his family like a man was supposed to.

19

Things between Asia and Josiah went from zero to one hundred in a matter of months. They quickly became fast friends and soon after, lovers. In a month, they were inseparable. If Josiah couldn't make it to Philadelphia during the week because he was busy, he always made it a priority to get there on the weekends to see her. Josiah borderline adored her. Asia was a beautiful person; inside and out. She was a good mother, had a great personality and was very caring. She always asked Josiah how his day went, if anything was bothering him, and even lent her ear when he needed to talk, as well as her shoulder if he needed one to cry. Several times she had even drove to Delaware to bring him food when he was too busy to eat, and even to bring him something as simple as cough medicine when he was sick. Josiah was a firm believer in being good to those that were good to him. For that reason, he spoiled Asia.

It had been a long time since someone came into Asia's life and treated her the way she dreamed of being treated. And for her, it wasn't even all about the money. Since Mitch was handling business on the inside, Asia didn't need any money.

However, anytime Josiah came around, he refused to let Asia spend a dime. Josiah had deep pockets, and Asia didn't realize it until that day.

"Babe why are you still in this hotel?" he asked groggily, after falling asleep on the uncomfortable couch. His legs dangled weirdly off the sofa. He stretched them to get the kinks out. After wiping his eyes, he glanced over to the bed; sure enough, Asia and her son were still sitting in the same spot watching cartoons. Although he usually slept in the bed with the two of them, he wanted to sleep with Asia alone. Hasan was approaching two years old, and in Josiah's opinion, he could sit in a safe, child-proof room and watch cartoons alone for a bit. Unfortunately, the suite was small and there was no other room to find privacy in, other than the bathroom. After becoming frustrated and Asia not seeming to notice, he dozed off on the couch.

Finally switching her gaze from the television to Josiah, she responded to his question. "Because, I'm still paying on this appeal Mitch is fighting for, and it normally takes half of the money he sends me. All a nigga got is hope, and I don't want to take that from him. Even though they're probably going to deny the appeal, I'm not going to tell him that. It's his money, so I spend it how he tells me."

"I understand that, but you can't keep living in a hotel. You gotta get a place. What's stopping you?"

"I don't know," she shrugged. "It's cheap and I like it here," she replied.

She paid under $2,000 a month to stay in Willow Grove at the extended stay. She didn't have a lease and she was quite comfortable. She had a little kitchen to cook, her own bathroom, a couch, and a bed for her and her son to sleep in comfortably. She knew a house was going to cost her an arm and a leg in the area, and she didn't really want to move into an apartment. So, she figured she would wait until she was ready to move.

Josiah rose up off the couch and looked around for his shoes. "Come on, get dressed," he said. "We 'bout to find you a spot." Her living in a hotel was a problem for him. One that could easily be fixed.

"Noooo, I don't feel like looking around. I'd have to get bank statements and all that," she complained.

"Why you need that?" he asked, with a light chuckle. "I'm going to buy you a house. How much you think you'll need? I can find you something for around $200k in cash, right?"

"What!" Asia said in surprise. "You're not gonna buy me a house," she laughed. *Or would he,* she wondered.

"Yes, I am," he stood there and looked at her. "I got you. I enjoy spending time with you and being with you. But, when I'm with you, I want to be comfortable. That couch," he frowned his face and pointed to it, "*that couch* is not comfortable," he laughed. "So, you get him ready and I'm going to go buy you your very first house."

Asia jumped off the bed, ran up to Josiah, and embraced him. "I'm really getting a house?" she asked. Although she knew Josiah had money, her brain wasn't registering that he had it like *that.* For him to be able to just spend a couple hundred thousand on a house was unheard of. To have a man spend that type of money on her felt surreal.

"You really are getting a house," he beamed. "Now, give me a kiss wit' ya sexy ass," he said, before kneeling down and pressing his lips against hers.

~

With Hasan in tow, Asia and Josiah looked around all day for a house. Real estate was expensive in the suburbs of Philadelphia; however, the prices didn't seem to faze Josiah. Before they began Asia's house hunt, Josiah drove them down to Wilmington, so that he could grab some cash out of his safe. His place was beautiful and overlooked the river. She wondered how much money Josiah really had. His place had to have costed several hundred thousand dollars.

While they drove back towards her home in Delaware, Asia looked online at real estate listings. She eventually stumbled upon a beautiful condo; however, it was a little overprices at $219k. Disregarding that fact, they still went to look at it. It was a two-bedroom, two-bathroom condo. The place was breathtakingly beautiful. To Josiah, it was a little small, with only 1,600 square feet of living space. His condo alone had 3,000 square feet. Nevertheless, he couldn't deny the fact that it was nice. The kitchen had been remodeled and now had beautiful gray cabinets with gold knobs. It also had granite countertops and stainless-steel appliances.

Despite the condo still needing more upgrades, Asia immediately fell in love with it. It was the perfect size for her and Hasan, and it was in the perfect location. Seeing her light up in the place immediately had Josiah sold. If she was happy, then so was he. With a duffle bag full of cash in his trunk, he was able to get the price down to $195k. That quickly, Asia became a homeowner.

UNTITLED

~

"Hayward! You have a legal visit," the officer said, leaning his head slightly into Mitch's cell. Mitch who was sitting at the desk in the room, put down the hookup he was eating. He got up and retrieved his sneakers from underneath the bed. After sliding them on his feet, he followed the guard down the stairs and off the tier.

He prayed his lawyer was coming with good news. He had been grinding for months and hoped all the money he was dishing out was helping the appeal process. The courts could deny the appeal request, or they could grant it, depending on what his lawyer's argument was. Any past technicalities or issues that occurred at the previous trial were all grounds for an appeal. For Mitch, it was his previous lawyers' incompetence. The last lawyer he had didn't address nor stress important issues that Mitch had asked him to. His argument was weak, and Mitch didn't feel like he was represented to the fullest capacity. Mitch continued through security, and entered a small room reserved for lawyers who were coming to meet wltli their clients. They called these legal visits.

His lawyer, a middle-aged Jewish man name Simon Bernosky, stood up to greet him as soon as he walked through the door.

"How are you doing Mitch?" he asked, shaking Mitch's hand. "It's nice to be able to put a face to a name," he said with a genuine smile while pushing his thin, wire glasses up on his nose.

Mitch noticed that he was in a pretty good mood. He hoped it was because he had some good news to tell him. He also noticed that he was impeccably dressed. He had on an Armani suit and a pair of Alessandro Demesure Leather Oxford's. Although Mitch was a street nigga, he was well acquainted with the finer things. A lot of his clients were part of the upper echelon in Philadelphia. He knew the shoes alone easily ran $1,500. Asia had gotten him one of the best lawyers in the city. He specialized in jury trials, as well as appeals. His firm had a reputation of defending *and winning* some of the toughest, most high-profile cases in the city. His last lawyer had been chosen by his mother. Asia had picked this one. She didn't tell him how she'd found him, but Mitch was glad that she had.

"Thanks for coming to see me," Mitch said, after letting go of his lawyer's hand. He sat down in the metal chair at the table, opposite of his lawyer. "Hopefully, you're here with some good news," he said. While he waited for an answer, the guard that had escorted him in, motioned for Mitch to lift his hands up. Once Mitch complied, he secured his cuffs to the table for security reasons.

"Well, I don't want to get too far ahead of myself he laughed." He noticed that Mitch didn't. Mitch didn't find the joke funny. He had been given a lot of time and didn't find anything amusing about staying there *or* possibly getting out. An appeal was his last hope.

"So, what can you tell me?" Mitch asked. Asia had given him over twenty racks. He expected results or some type of news.

"Well, I reviewed the case and I agree with you that your previous lawyer should have argued more about the fact that it was a robbery attempt. I mean, the fact that you were able to escape with your life is unbelievable. The twenty bullet-holes to your car; the numerous shell-casings; all of this should have been argued relentlessly and beat into the head of every juror there."

"Right," Mitch said, feeling a little hopeful. "All the nigga kept saying is, he didn't want to shed too much light on the fact that they were trying to rob me for drug money. He didn't want them to lack sympathy because I was a drug dealer and was breaking the law to begin with."

"Well, I can see what he meant on that note. Yet, it's important. I say present the facts but highlight the details. They may not sympathize with you because you are a drug dealer, but they can't dispute that you are human and that you were literally fighting for your life. Drug dealer or not, you were scared, adrenaline kicked in and it was either kill ... or be killed."

"So, what next?" Mitch asked.

"I'm going to have my assistant draft up your appeal request papers, and I'll get this right over to the judge. You will hear something in a few weeks; hopefully sooner."

"Okay," he said. His lawyer motioned for the officer to come back in, so Mitch could be uncuffed from the table. Once he did that, Mitch got up and exhaled deeply. For the first time in a very long time, he felt hope.

20

"I'm not taking a plea. That shit is out of the question," Waleek said firmly.

It was seven o'clock a.m. and he was beyond irritated. His lawyer had gotten him the fuck out of his bed to come see him early in the morning to tell him some shit that could have waited until the afternoon. It was the end of summer and the stuff jail cell made it difficult for him to sleep. With no air-conditioner, Waleek tossed and turned all night.

"It's either that, or you take it to a jury trial," his lawyer said. "And we've gone over that. If you take it to jury trial, your child's mother, Maleeka, will be called to the stand to testify," his lawyer said.

He waited in his chair uncomfortably for Waleek to respond. His client wasn't the easiest man to deal with. Considering the circumstances, he did his best to empathize. Nevertheless, Waleek's sour demeanor and disposition didn't necessarily put him at ease.

Waleek's body stiffened up and his face changed to a scowl at the mention of Muff's name. The first chance he got, he planned to pin her against a wall and break her fucking neck.

He had been sitting in jail several months before he even found out that she had been lying to him about talking to the police. Never once did she admit that she'd thrown him under the bus and gave them information. Not *some* information ... but all of it! Thinking there were no eye-witnesses willing to testify, his lawyer pushed for a Motion of Discovery so he could see what other weak-ass evidence and statements they had against him. Assuming there were no willing witnesses, their next step was going to be asking for a dismissal. Imagine his shock when he found out that Muff had identified him at the scene. Waleek was not only disappointed, he was livid. As crazy as Muff acted over him, she showed her true feelings. She didn't give a damn about him; she cared about herself.

Although Waleek understood Muff was scared due to the circumstances surrounding the homicide, she should have kept her mouth closed, or at least been honest about what she said. That way he and his lawyer would have been prepared to plan their defense. Initially, they were going to go with he didn't do it, now they had no choice but to go with self-defense. As much as he despised his baby-mother at this point, he needed her to reinforce that claim.

"Couldn't she just retract her statement?" Waleek asked. The last thing he wanted was for Muff's simple ass to get on the stand.

"Yeah, but the state's attorney isn't going to buy that. They'll still subpoena her to come to court. And what about if another eye-witness surfaces? I was under the impression that prosecution is still trying to get the statements of the two young men that were with him. Anything can between now and trial. One of them could get busted for something else. That's all the state's attorney would need as leverage to get their statements."

Waleek nodded his head in agreement. His lawyer had a solid point. That was something he didn't want to take his chances on. "Self-defense it is," he said.

Waleek's lawyer nodded in satisfaction and began gathering up his paperwork. After his departure, the officer that had brought Waleek in, uncuffed him from the metal table that he was seated at. After being escorted back to his tier, he waited patiently to use the phone. Luckily, it was still early so there wasn't much of a wait. On the weekends, it wasn't unusual to wait hours to use the phone. An hour later, when one finally became free, Waleek scurried to it to call Muff. She answered on the sixth ring.

"What the fuck took you so long to answer the phone?" Waleek said angrily as soon as the call connected. He hadn't even given her the opportunity to say anything.

"Hello to you too, Waleek," she responded dryly.

Muff didn't feel like his shit today. She glanced at the time on her phone. It was barely nine o'clock in the morning. She wouldn't even have answered the call if she didn't need more money for Kayla. Since Waleek had been gone, things had gotten extremely hard for her. Without his massive financial support, Muff couldn't afford the house she had recently moved into; she barely had enough to keep her, or their daughter up. She had already terminated her lease on her apartment in Germantown, so her subsidized housing was gone. Even if she hadn't terminated it, they probably would have evicted her anyway. Zee had been killed right on her doorstep, and all the cameras scattered throughout the complex showed that Zee and his murderer were both her unauthorized visitors.

When Waleek left, she didn't have a dime saved up. The couple hundred dollars in her purse was nothing more than food and gas money. The new house she moved into didn't last but a month. As soon as the second month's rent was due, Muff had no way to pay it. With no high school diploma, there was no job around that would pay her enough to even put a dent in the rent; so, she didn't even bother looking for one. Although she still fucked niggas, most of them were broke and barely getting by. They damn sure didn't have money like Waleek did. He should feel lucky that she was even answering his call. Why the fuck should she after he basically gave all his money to a bitch she despised? A bitch that also wasted no time turning her back on him as soon as the opportunity presented himself. Carolyn still gave Muff money when Waleek approved it; however, she regulated that shit like the government. Only giving her what she needed for Kayla and nothing more. Rising from her bed, she sat up to hear what Waleek was talking about.

"Why the fuck you ain't up?" Waleek asked. "You stay complaining about not having any money but every time I call, you sleep or bullshitting."

"Waleek, I don't wanna hear that shit! What da fuck you want nigga? Ya daughter wasn't feeling well last night and I was up late as fuck because she complained all night about a damn stomachache," she responded impatiently.

"Whatever," Waleek said, brushing her off. Every time Muff didn't like something he said, she would somehow figure out a way to involve his daughter. "Well, did you give her something for it? Is she feeling better?" he asked. Although he couldn't stand Muff, he loved his daughter.

"Yeah she alright. She finally managed to fall asleep so hopefully it was just a little bug or something."

"Good. Keep me posted. But look, check this out. I'm not gonna hold you up and shit ... You gon' have to get on the stand," he said bluntly.

"How the fuck I'm gon' do that Waleek? You told me not to say shit else to the police and now you want me to get on the stand. If I do that, they're still going to question me and repeat all the shit I said in the beginning."

"You shouldn't have fuckin' said shit!" Waleek yelled, losing his patience. He took a deep breath. He hadn't called to argue, and frankly, he needed her at this point.

"I told you how they came at me Waleek," Muff said, becoming defensive. "They started talking about locking me up and charging me as an accessory. There's cameras every-fuck-ing-where out here. You know damn well you was gon' be all over them," she said angrily.

Waleek inhaled and exhaled to try and regain his patience. He was angry, and at times, he couldn't control it. He also couldn't help but blame Muff behind his misfortunes. Although he knew he too was at fault, he mostly blamed her. Not only was she fucking another nigga and still taking his money, she allowed him to head over there, knowing she had another nigga there. All she did was play games and bring drama into his life. Worst of all, she completely dismantled and destroyed his relationship he had with Asia. After being initially charged and speaking with Asia, she seemed to be completely on board to rock with him. She showed no signs of hostility, despite what they had went through previously. As soon as Muff realized Asia was going to be handling his money, she called her and told her everything. She told her about the house he'd just helped her get; about all the money he had been giving her; about everything that led up to Zee's murder; and worse, the baby that she didn't even fucking keep! That one phone call literally destroyed his state-of-mind.

Asia left him and never looked back. Even though she took a significant portion of his money, he didn't blame her. After everything he'd put her through with Muff, she deserved it. Despite her anger and animosity towards him, she still took care of his lawyer right away. Asia had stopped answering his calls the day she revealed that Muff had told her everything. Despite that, she still made sure he had the best, most high-profile attorney in the city. He respected that. She had done the noble thing. Even after he had done her wrong, she still refused to completely shit on him. He was bitter and angry with himself. And he couldn't help but admit that he borderline hated Muff's ass.

"Yeah, the police and state's attorney always lie about everything Muff. You from the hood. We've been taught that since we were little kids. You know damn well you can't trust them motherfucker's," he said doing his best to keep from growing annoyed. "You see how they do on First 48," he reminded her. He hated even talking to Muff's stupid ass. If she weren't sitting on the phone lying, she was making up excuses about why she did the dumb shit she did.

"I know Waleek. For the millionth time, I fucked up," she said.

"Yeah, you did ... Look, you gotta get on the stand. The only argument my lawyer thinks we have a chance of winning is self-defense. Yeah, they're going to question you but you gotta tell them the truth that way they will hopefully rule in my favor. They jumped on me and Zee pulled the gun."

"Waleek I didn't see—"

He instantly cut her off. Every call was monitored and recorded. "Don't say shit else on this phone," he demanded. "My lawyer will brief you, so you'll be prepared for court. I'm gonna tell him you're on board and he will call you soon," Waleek stated with finality. Muff had no choice. She got him in this mess, and she was going to help get him out.

"Okay," Muff said reluctantly.

After arranging for Muff to pick up a couple hundred dollars from his mom, they hung up, with Waleek promising to call back in a few days. Waleek placed the phone down in the designated slot and walked back to his cell. If by the grace of God, he made it home, he vowed to get his daughter and never fuck with Muff again in his life. He also vowed to try and reconnect with Asia. He'd spoke to a few of his young boys and he hadn't heard of her hooking up with anyone else. He knew that Mitch was going to be down for a while, so he figured Asia was likely still single. Even though he had done her wrong, he loved her and wanted to be with her. Hopefully, she found it in her heart to forgive him.

WALEEK STOOD in the noisy lunch line and waited to get his food. The cafeteria was all the way at the bottom of the jail in the basement. It was the only place they could accommodate that number of inmates at one time. The line moved quickly, and before he knew it, he had his metal tray extended out, so the inmates working the chow line could place the specified food item down on it. Waleek looked down. Today they were having sloppy joes, tater tots and green beans. It looked repulsive. He hated the jail food; the shit was borderline sickening. Unfit for consumption. Nevertheless, he had to eat to survive, so he took his tray and sat down at a nearby table where he knew a few niggas.

"Wassup?" Waleek said casually to everyone at the table. He placed his tray down and went to sit but was abruptly stopped.

"You can't sit here fam." The man speaking to him was short and fat. His name was Quentin. Waleek didn't know him that well, but he knew him well enough for them to greet one another and be cordial.

"What?" Waleek said, as if he didn't understand what Quentin meant. He released his tray and stood fully back to his feet. That way, if shit popped off, he wouldn't be at a disadvantage.

"You can't sit here," Quentin reiterated, this time using a more forceful tone.

"Says who?" Waleek asked, his eyebrows going up. He glanced around to see if anyone was watching. Sure enough, they were. He quickly glanced at the other three men at the table. He sensed their reluctance. Waleek already knew what this stemmed from, as well as what it was leading to.

"Says all of us," Quentin responded, speaking for everyone. "We don't fuck with rats. They don't sit with us, *and* they don't eat with us."

The other three niggas at the table stared at Waleek. They hated that it had come to this, but it hadn't been their call. Rumors were circulating through the jail that Waleek had snitched. Someone had seen his name on some paperwork. Snitching wasn't honorable. In the jail and prison system, it got you bullied, extorted, and oftentimes killed.

"Matter of fact ... rats don't eat period," Quentin said. He placed his hand on Waleek's tray and slid it towards him. "This mine now," he said.

Waleek stood there for a second, and before he knew it, he had snatched up the tray from the table, and smacked Quentin viciously across the face with it. The act shocked everyone at that table and the surrounding ones as well. Oftentimes, the "rat" label was associated with cowardice.

Nigga's got me fucked up, Waleek thought, as he proceeded to deliver a brutal beating to Quentin, for his outlandish and brazen act of disrespect. The other three men watched in utter surprise as Waleek repeatedly slammed his tray down into Quentin's face. They didn't care much for him to begin with. It had been his idea to try and bully Waleek. He was now on his own. They had upcoming court cases and didn't want to be sitting in the hole behind a nigga they really didn't fuck with.

The smirk Quentin once wore on his face, had now been replaced by a long, deep gash that leaked blood profusely. For nearly thirty-seconds, Waleek took out all his anger on Quentin. He also wanted to make an example out of him, just in case someone else wanted to get out of line and attempt to disrespect him again. He didn't want anyone to think for a second that his reasoning to point the finger at Ricardo had anything to do with him being a coward.

To Waleek, it was a dog eat dog world, where only the strong survived. It was then that he decided he would have to become vicious in order to survive. He knew this act was just one of many to come. He just had to prepare himself for it. Waleek knew that this bid was going to be different. He was going to fight the case with everything he had. Something told him that this experience was going to change him; he was going to return to the streets a completely different man.

21

With his weary eyes focused on the road, Ethan reached down and grabbed his open can of Red Bull. Bringing the top to his lips, he tilted the can back and allowed the sweet and tangy liquid to flow into his mouth and down his throat. He was tired and was doing his absolute best to stay awake. Ethan was a twenty-one-year-old college student that worked as a delivery driver for Sweet Treats Bakery. The job paid exceptionally well, but he hated the long hours required. His shift had started at eight o'clock a.m. and it was now six o'clock p.m., and he was still driving. He had one last run to make to a car dealership out in Dover, Delaware. Apparently, they were having some sort of event the following day and needed a rush order for ten boxes of pastries. Ethan didn't understand why it simply couldn't wait until the next day; however, he did as he was instructed. The boss wanted them delivered that day, so he was now in route to Dover to get the order delivered.

Ethan yawned loudly as he sat his can of Red Bull back down in the cup holder. He wasn't far from his destination. Once he dropped the boxes off, it would only take him forty-five minutes to get back to Wilmington, drop the van off, and head home. He glanced at the clock. 6:03 p.m. shown brightly on the display. Yawning loudly again, he hit cruise control and paced his speed at 65 miles-per-hour. Something told him not to do it; but he did it anyway. Something told him to open the window to let in a cool breeze, but he didn't do that either. Somewhere during his drive, while holding the steering wheel, sleep overcame him. His unconscious mind caused his eyes to flutter and then ultimately shut. Ethan fell asleep at the wheel. Ethan couldn't have been sleep more than ten seconds. When he realized what had happened, the bakery van had spun off the road and now lay upside down in a grassy field right off the highway.

ETHAN WAS SO scared when he woke up and realized he had flipped the company van. He was even more scared when the fire department freed him from the mangled vehicle, and he was placed under arrest before being put into the ambulance. He didn't know what he was under arrest for. Last time he checked; people got into accidents every day. That didn't make them criminals. Things all started to make more sense when he was cleared by the hospital, and subsequently taken to the local police department for questioning. Terror swept through him when the officers introduced themselves as part of the narcotics department.

"Were you aware that you were riding with ten bricks of Heroin in your delivery van?" they asked.

"For the hundredth time, no I did not!" Ethan yelled, growing frustrated. "I didn't fuckin' know!" he argued. He had been in the same spot, answering the same questions for the past couple of hours. He was exhausted, hungry, and he had to use the bathroom. He honestly felt like they were violating his rights, but he didn't say anything; he just wanted to get out of there.

"Well, who do you work for?" the Caucasian, freckled-face detective asked him for the tenth time.

Ethan ran his fingers through his blonde hair in frustration and huffed. "I told you ... Sweet Treats Bakery. I know you seen it on the side of the van," he said sarcastically.

"Look, Ethan," the woman officer said softly.

She was a young, attractive, African American cop; probably in her late twenties. "We know you work for Sweet Treats Bakery. What we really need to know is who put the drugs in the van. Who sent you down here transporting drugs through our town? Now ... You're an intelligent fella. You seem to be on the right path. We checked your wallet and see you're a student at the University of Delaware. Don't fuck up your life behind some drug-dealing lowlife. Tell us who's drugs these are. Who would send a young kid down the road with ten kilos of dope? You're looking at a lot of time," she said with emphasis.

Although Ethan didn't know it, they were playing good cop, bad cop.

"Tell us something and we might be able to let you walk out of here; but, if you can't tell us anything, we're going to have to charge you with it," she said with finality before pushing her shoulder-length hair behind her ear.

She hoped what she was saying to the young boy, was sinking in. In her heart, she didn't think he knew anything at all. They all had their fingers crossed that he did, however. If he could tell them something, that would be one of the biggest drug busts the town had ever seen.

"I don't know," he said, before burying his head into his hands and sobbing loudly. "I just want to go home. Please let me just call my grandmother and my boss," he continued to sob.

He was exhausted and had a class first thing in the morning. His grandmother was going to be pissed if she had to cover his rent and books again the following semester. She already had it hard; taking care of him since he was ten years old. Both his parents had been hooked on Heroin and wound up losing custody of him. The last he knew; they both were still running the streets of Wilmington getting high.

The delivery job at Sweet Treats had been a break for him. He had been working there for nearly a year and hadn't had any complaints about the place. He got paid good money, and they usually worked with him around his school schedule. However, he did notice that business had picked up tremendously. With a full-time course load, he was having trouble keeping up at the job. They still needed him to work full-time hours, even though he was barely getting sleep. Instead of cutting his hours, they offered him more money. His manager, a black lady named Trish, said they didn't have the proper staff to cut his hours, while still getting all the deliveries out on time. They needed him.

Recently, he also noticed that he was making a lot more runs to Philadelphia and Dover. More than he ever had before. Now that he thought about it; something fishy had to be going on. He suddenly became angry that he had been thrust in the middle of their conspiracy to sell a shitload of drugs. He had to think! Was there anything unusual that he had noticed? *Come on. Think, think, think*, he said to himself. Then he remembered!

"There's a black guy that comes in there a lot," Ethan said, lifting his head out of his hands. "He usually places large orders. A couple of times I helped at the counter and saw him there. A few months ago, ... I saw him in a uniform. He was driving one of the delivery vans. I was surprised because I always thought he was just a customer."

He hoped that information helped. He really didn't know anything else. However, there was no doubt in his mind now, that there was some shady shit going on at the bakery.

"Are you able to describe him?" the white, male cop asked him.

Ethan began to describe they guy he remember seeing, while the white cop took notes. "He's tall. Probably around six foot two or maybe, six foot three. He's brown-skinned. He's a clean-cut guy. He has tattoos up and down both arms," he continued.

"But you've never seen him handle drugs or deliver drugs to the bakery?" the black cop named Tara asked.

"No, I haven't," he said solemnly. He prayed he was giving them enough information so that he could get out of there and go home.

"Is there anything else you can tell us?" they asked.

"No," he said. He really wished he had more to give them, but he didn't.

"Okay." The two officers gathered up their notepads and coffee cups. After advising Ethan that they were stepping out for a minute, they left, and stood outside of the door.

They huddled together with another detective from the precinct and spoke quietly. They believed Ethan was telling the truth. They knew he didn't know much; however, they felt like he could be an asset. Through the glass window beside the door, they studied Ethan. They could see him, but he couldn't see them. He was scared. He kept running his fingers through his hair and he was visibly shaken.

"He's either going to have to help us, or we have to charge him with something. That's way too much drugs coming through for no one to be charged," the detective stated.

He too was handling the case; however, because of the large quantity of drugs associated with the case, he had been on the phone with the Feds. They were on their way to speak with Ethan. He had no doubt that they would probably pick up the case. Opening the door, all three detectives walked back into the room.

"Ethan. The Feds are on their way to speak with you. I'm Detective Ryan Cole. I haven't had the pleasure of meeting you." Detective Cole was a gray-haired older white man. He extended his thin, wrinkly hand so Ethan could shake it.

"I figured I would go ahead and introduce myself before the Feds come in and take over. So, I want to be frank," he said, looking at Ethan with a grim look on his face. He wanted him to understand that this was serious business.

"Soon, this case is going to be out of our hands. We figured; we might as well advise you of a couple of things before they get here. They found ten kilos of Heroin in that van Ethan. With that number of drugs, someone must be charged. If you can't help us more, that someone is going to be you. If you choose to help as much as you can, you'll probably be asked to find out more information. Part of that will require you to wear a wire," he said. He stood there, his emotionless face studying Ethan. "I know it sucks, but somehow, someway, you got yourself mixed up with some shady people."

"Fuck," Ethan murmured, before burying his head back down in his hands. There was no way in Hell he was taking a charge for ten kilos. What other choice did he have?

22

The very next morning, Josiah leaned over and pressed his lips into Asia's to wake her up. A wide smile crept along her face as her eyes peeled open and realized it was her fine ass man. She blinked to make sure she wasn't dreaming. She had been in her new place for several weeks, and every now and then, she couldn't believe things were real. She had gone from living in a shitty ass apartment, on a shitty ass block with her mama; to living in her own condo, that had been bought and paid for in *cash*. She had also gone from unemployed and trying to steal bus rides to make an interview, to owning her own daycare center. God was good. She had her own cash, own income, and not one, but two nigga's who took care of her.

Mitch was still sending money every month and Josiah made sure she didn't want for anything. Not only did she have her own condo in nearby Elkins Park; Josiah had also upgraded her four-year-old BMW to a brand-new Mercedes Benz GLB250. Life wasn't good; it was fucking great.

Asia's tired eyes fluttered back open after hearing Josiah call her name several times softly. Josiah had been staying there at her new place for about a week now, and Asia was loving every bit of it. She loved waking up against his big, beautiful tattooed body. Loved waking up to his smiles and kisses. He was so thoughtful; so attentive. He did everything in his power to relax her and make her feel good. He also did everything to make her feel wanted, needed, and cared for. Random kisses, back massages, breakfast in bed, gifts, nights out and most importantly, hot spontaneous sex. Josiah surprised her with everything he could think of, as often as possible.

She couldn't believe he had come into her life and wanted her; more like, adored her. He was also good to Hasan, even though he had no kids of his own. She wanted to be with Josiah, and a strong part of her could see herself building with him, having babies by him, and having a long bomb-ass life together. The only problem was, she wasn't sure how the fuck she was going to tell Mitch.

Josiah had been pressing her for weeks to inform Mitch of their relationship; however, Asia was hesitant. She didn't want to disappoint Mitch, nor hurt him. Josiah was his friend, and they had crossed the line by becoming intimate in the first place. There was no doubt in her mind that Mitch was going to be pissed. He was a man of principle, and some people and things were simply considered off limits. Josiah, however, didn't see it that way. To him, Mitch may not like it, but he would respect it. He had to respect the fact that a real nigga had stepped into his girl and son's life. Mitch knew what caliber of man he was. He knew his girl and son would be provided for, loved, and protected. Any real nigga would respect that.

"Good morning babe," Asia said, still smiling. She quickly shook the thoughts of Mitch and switched her focus to the man in front of her. She sat up in her bed and leaned against the headboard. To her surprise, Hasan was nestled to Josiah's side, on his back and fast asleep.

"What's he doing in here?" she asked with a hoarse laugh.

She quickly put her hand to her mouth and cleared her throat. "Did he get out of his bed?"

"Naaaahhhh. He was up before us, so I went and got him. You know he do the most in the morning. Start kicking the wall, banging his toys and shit," he laughed as he scrolled through his iPhone.

Asia couldn't help but smile. She loved how Josiah treated Hasan. She glanced over at him and he looked so peaceful.

"Why didn't you lay him in the middle?" she asked.

"Cuz ... Lil' nigga can't have you *all* to himself," he laughed. "I'm trying to teach him how to share early. But look at this," he said with a smile. He passed his phone to her so she could look at what he had pulled up on his screen.

Asia took the phone and saw that he had made reservations to Hotel Casa del Mar, a hotel in Santa Monica, California. The pictures he had pulled up were beautiful. She was sure that the place was even more beautiful in real life. Asia's eyes instantly lit up. "Are we going?" she asked. She had to ask; Josiah was always so spontaneous and full of surprises. He said the trait came from his mother who stayed on the move. She hadn't yet met her, but Josiah always spoke highly of her and promised Asia that they would meet soon.

"Yeah, we're going if you down. We can go wherever you want," he reminded her. "But for this trip, just say the word, and I'll book it. I heard it's beautiful. Sits right on the beach," he said.

He loved the beach and he loved Asia. He figured she'd be the perfect person to enjoy the trip with.

"I want to go!" she said, smiling brightly. She leaned over and kissed him softly. She moaned as she pulled away. *This man does something to me. How did I get so lucky*, she thought. "Alright, don't start nothing," she whispered with a seductive wink.

His presence literally did something to her spirit. It was more than just him fucking her good. He did that very well. Her and Josiah connected deeply. Almost on a spiritual level. She too was a firm believer in fate. She had no doubt that Josiah had been sent to fill a part of her. To fill the void that Mitch had left. If only they didn't have those tremendous obstacles in their way. Asia glanced back over at Hasan who was still sleeping.

"That's you," he said, responding to Asia's remark.

Anything could get Asia fired up. It didn't take much. When it came to Josiah, she was always ready to go.

"I'm going to book this trip for this weekend. You think you can get a sitter for Hasan on such a short notice?" he asked. He waited for her to respond. He didn't want to hit the book button, if she was unsure about a sitter.

"A sitter?" she asked in surprise. "Why can't Hasan go?" she asked.

Josiah crinkled up his face playfully. "Why would you want to take a two-year-old to an intimate, luxury hotel, way out in California?" he asked.

Josiah loved Hasan but he didn't want to take a baby on a romantic getaway. He could only imagine what a hassle it would be just to fly with him.

Asia sighed. "I mean ... I could ask his grandmother, but I don't want her in my business. My mother ... is out of the question. We don't have a good relationship," she admitted. She hadn't filled Josiah in completely on her strained and toxic relationship with her mother.

"Why don't you want to ask Mitch's mom? You said yourself that they were great with Hasan and that they helped you out a lot."

He peered at her suspiciously and waited for her to respond. He was now curious. When she didn't respond, he continued. "You don't want Mitch finding out you're going on a trip?" he asked.

"It's not that," she paused. *It really was that*, but she wasn't going to let Josiah know it. She had expressed on several occasions that she didn't want Mitch finding out that she was seeing him romantically. She didn't understand why he couldn't seem to grasp that concept.

"Well then ... What is it?" he asked. He didn't understand why the hell she was always so concerned with getting Mitch's approval about everything.

Before Asia could respond, her phone began ringing. She leaned over and grabbed it from off the nightstand directly beside her bed. She glanced at the number. It was Mitch.

"I gotta take this. It's Mitch," she said.

She pushed the covers off her body and rose up from the bed. Josiah immediately became irritated. The shit with Mitch was getting on his nerves. They were grown and shouldn't have to tiptoe around anyone. He didn't understand what the big secret was. Mitch wasn't coming home for twenty years. He had told Josiah on more than one occasion that he wanted Asia to find a real nigga and be happy.

What the fuck am I, Josiah thought. He was a real nigga and had money longer than train smoke. He loved Asia and could take care of them with no problem. He also knew that Mitch was a man of principle. He would respect honesty. The longer they kept him in the dark, the worse it was going to be when Mitch found out. If Asia didn't tell Mitch soon, he was going to do it himself. He was a grown ass man. He wasn't about to baby step around no nigga, nor would he compromise his integrity. Asia was his girl now, not Mitch's.

"Hey Mitch. Good morning to you," she said into the phone. Josiah shot Asia a look that expressed his displeasure with the entire situation. He couldn't help the feeling of jealousy that was traveling in his veins.

Josiah looked back down at his phone and closed out of the hotel's reservation site. The mini vacation could wait. Just as he was exiting the website, he heard Asia gasp. He looked up and she had her hand to her mouth. She looked like she was in shock, and almost at a loss for words.

"You're fuckin' lying," she said slowly to Mitch. "What ... How?" she asked, nearly stammering over her words. Josiah continued looking at her. His expression had changed to one of concern.

"Yeah. Yeah. Okay," she nodded. "I'll get up with him and tell him. I'll be there first thing in the morning," she said, still looking like she was in shock. "Yeah. Okay. I love you too," she said.

Asia hung up the phone and stood there for a second with her phone gripped tightly in the palm of her hands.

"What the fuck happened?" Josiah asked.

Asia paused then looked at him. She was happy, but she had a wave of other feelings swirling through her body at the same time.

"Mitch got approved for an appeal." She stood there and stared at Josiah.

"What?" he asked, suddenly becoming stiff. He had an idea where this conversation was headed.

"The lawyer got him a bail while he awaits his new trial. His bail is $100k cash. He told me to ask you for $50,000 of it. I'll put up the rest."

Asia paused and swallowed the hard lump that had formed in her throat. Her heart was racing while her mind was processing thoughts at a mile a minute. She was borderline ecstatic, but she was also confused, overwhelmed, and crushed all at the same time.

What the hell is going to happen with Josiah and I, she thought to herself while staring at his shocked handsome face. Mitch was her baby-daddy, but her and Josiah were together. They were a couple. He had just bought her a house. He said he loved her and wanted to spend the rest of his life with her. She had no doubt that he meant every word of it. Josiah was a man's man. Things were about to get complicated. She didn't see Josiah sitting back and allowing Mitch to come in and reclaim his position in her life so easily. *Fuck, we should have been told him*, she thought, her mind still racing. However, she was now confused. She still loved Mitch. He had always taken care of her. She knew her life would be happy if she were with him as well. She knew that's what Mitch was going to expect when he got out; for them to pick up where they left off. Especially because he was under the impression that she was single. She didn't know what she was going to do.

She looked back over at Josiah, who was now sitting up in the bed with a blank expression on his face. He too was still at a loss for words.

"Mitch will be home tomorrow," she repeated so it could thoroughly sink in.

TEXTING LIST

To stay up to date on new releases, plus get exclusive information on contests, sneak peeks, and more...

Text ColeHartSig to (855)231-5230

www.ingramcontent.com/pod-product-compliance
Lightning Source LLC
Chambersburg PA
CBHW020543160726

47991CB00002B/560